THE WIND BEFORE RAIN

Dragons of Introvertia Book Two

By

James and Bit Barringer

ASIN B089655K6M
ISBN 9798674657552

Cover design by Marshall Daley
@onetruehazard on Instagram

www.DragonsOfIntrovertia.com

Table of Contents

ONE

Spring mornings were still cold this far to the north, Denavi Kiresti thought miserably. She shivered as she marched in step behind the rest of Saber Company, her black boots crunching on the hard ground while the scouts at the front picked their way through the dense oak trees and rolling hills of this no-man's-land between her home nation of Claira, the kingdom of Telravia to the west, and Introvertia to the southwest.

Saber Company's commanding officer, Captain Thiari Lanian, held up her hand and all eighty-two soldiers, mages, and healers came to a halt behind her. The company had sustained heavy casualties in a fight with the Telravians a week ago; the previous captain had been killed, along with around twenty others. Denavi had tried her best to save them, but she was only seventeen years old and hadn't even graduated from combat training yet. Her healing magic was nowhere near as strong as it would be one day. She *knew* that, but *knowing* hadn't made it hurt any less as she'd held that soldier's hand tightly, trying in vain to stem the flow of blood from his stomach as he'd screamed in pain and terror –

And besides, "only seventeen" wasn't as good an excuse now as it had been a few weeks ago. Oh, she'd heard the rumors, alright; it was impossible for any Clairan not to have heard the tales of that fifteen-year-old Introvertian boy who had teamed up with an Exclaimovian girl only a year older than him to steal back hundreds of dragons that the Exclaimovians were attempting to turn into their own army. At least, that's what the rumors from the Exclaimovian traders had said; their government wasn't officially admitting anything, which meant either that was the truth or else the truth was even *worse.* The other rumor was that the Introvertian kid – technically he was an adult in their kingdom, but that was beside the point – had somehow learned magic along the way, and had taken his newfound power back to his kingdom. Magic, in Introvertia again! Yes, it was illegal there for the moment, but what if...

"Introvertia is going to attack us with their new magic," Clairans had whispered to each other confidentially. "I hear they're planning their first assault already."

And Denavi believed it. She'd never met an Introvertian, but Claira's allies in the kingdom of Esteria told them that Introvertians were quiet, shrewd, scheming people, the kind who would smile to your face while they stabbed you in the back. "You can't trust an Introvertian," one Esterian had told her a few years before. "Exclaimovians, they'll at least tell you what they're thinking. But Introvertians just keep it all in. They listen and listen and then pow! They use what you said against you. Don't ever trust one, Denavi. You might not live long enough to regret it."

Now these people had magic to go along with their dragons.

Maybe that's where Saber Company was going, Denavi thought with a thrill of excitement. There was no way Claira would attack Introvertia with a single under-strength company, but maybe her unit was on a scouting mission, or maybe they would meet up with other companies to attack some Introvertian fortress. Daydreaming wouldn't accomplish anything, but it was way better than thinking about how cold she was and how much she'd rather be at home reading poetry.

No, I can't think that, she scolded herself. Clairan society worshiped the ideal of the Noble Enlightened Warrior. The poetry was fine, but if anyone knew there was somewhere she'd rather be than on the battlefield, that would bring shame to her family – well, her mother. Her father had been killed in honorable warfare against those savages from the Kingdom of Vagran to the north eight years before. She pushed her chin-length black hair back behind her ears, then pulled her knit cap down lower.

There was a murmur of activity at the front of the company now, and Captain Lanian appeared moments later, whispering orders. "Telravians again," someone in front of her said, and Denavi's blood ran colder than it already was. Telravia was a brutal society where the strongest spellcasters were revered and almost worshiped. The pursuit of magical power was the most important thing to them. Denavi had even heard from some Esterians – she didn't know if it was true, but she believed it – that Telravia was ruled by a council of seven sorcerers, and that the only way to get a seat on the council was to kill one of the members and take their spot. And their fighting style...

Denavi shivered.

Introvertians had dragons, and Claira used several kinds of magical creatures, mostly giant falcons and arctic tigers, the strongest of which even had some spellcasting abilities of their own. But Telravia used creatures that looked like they'd been stitched together from nightmares: horrors and abominations and things that might have been ghosts. The sorcerers themselves were skilled in the most advanced forms of primal magic, sniping from the rear while those battle horrors did the up-close fighting. Claira usually won those battles, but at horrible cost.

The Telravians were marching along a little-used

sunken road, not far from where the Clairans were hiding. There were only forty of the enemy, which was still plenty enough to do serious damage, but if the Clairans could strike hard and fast –

There was no more time for thought because now they were standing, marching to the top of the slope that led down to the sunken road, and then they were over the top, the infantry screaming a battle cry as they sprinted with their swords out. Lances of purple energy exploded out from the surprised Telravians and some of the Clairans fell in mid-stride, bodies tumbling down the hill. Other lances hit the ground and sent clouds of dirt bursting into the air, or made trees evaporate into sawdust. Screams filled the forest, but the Clairan vanguard kept surging forward. "Death before dishonor!" Captain Lanian shouted, and all the soldiers behind her echoed, "Death before dishonor!"

Denavi heard her own voice shouting, "Death before dishonor!"

Clairan spellcasters had gotten their own view of the battlefield now, their elemental magic sending fireballs and arcs of lightning toward the Telravians. Some kind of magical shield deflected a number of the spells up into the trees; Denavi saw one lightning bolt smash an ancient red oak and the tree immediately caught fire, sending up smoke that began to block out the blue sky –

But there were the Clairan battle falcons, wheeling out of the air and descending toward the Telravian front lines. They were almost as tall as Introvertian dragons were said to be, waist-high to a grown Clairan, their wings cocked back as they swooped down in attack. A deep rhythmic thud echoed through the valley, and huge plumes of ash-gray magic shot skyward. Immediately a dozen falcons were caught by the blasts, bursting into feathers or spiraling to the ground with broken wings. The Telravians gave a horrible cheer of victory and the Clairans fell back momentarily.

Then an even more ghastly sound erupted from the far hill, and suddenly the valley was filled with Telravian abominations, gray-white creatures that looked like they used to be human but were now just burned-out shells. Denavi didn't know what foul dark magic had created them, and she didn't care. "Healer!" someone cried from halfway down the hillside, and Denavi charged forward, pretending a bravery that she didn't truly feel, skidding to a halt next to a man who had been pierced through the shoulder by a purple lance of primal energy.

"Am I going to die?" the soldier asked.

"Not today," Denavi assured him, tearing his shirt away from the wound. She began working the counter-magic healing spell; warm energy bubbled up inside her stomach, then through her arms and into her hands. Her palms began to glow golden-white, and immediately the soldier's wound began to close – although Denavi and the other healers had found that this Telravian magic never truly healed all the way. The soldier would have a pocked scar on his shoulder for life, although he *should* regain full use of the limb sooner or later...

The battle still raged on the sunken road; Clairan infantry had slain most of the Telravian horrors, but the swords and the magic were still thick. Smoke was beginning to darken the valley, from the spells and from the burning tree, and flying dirt had landed on everyone. Denavi could hardly tell friend from enemy anymore. She knew she was supposed to hurl herself into the middle of the fight, looking for more people to heal – *death before dishonor* – but –

Suddenly a purple lance – weak, flickering, as if the Telravian who cast it were dying – smashed into Denavi's side just below her ribcage. Gasping in pain, she crumpled to her knees, then rolled onto her back. *So this is what it feels like. This is why they always ask if they're going to die.* Looking up through the haze of smoke and debris, her breath coming in ragged gasps, she forced the healing magic to bubble within her, placing her hands on her side. There was blood – *MY blood,* she thought. Panic rose in her again, and her teeth began to chatter as she focused the spell one more time, willing herself to concentrate on the feel of the healing power inside her.

She heard a magical tone rip through the air, a sound she recognized from the previous week: the Telravians were sounding the retreat. The few that were left fled up the far hill while their remaining horrors covered the flanks. The Clairans did not pursue. Denavi forced herself to stand, wobbling, trying to find her footing so she could make her way to the sunken road and help any who were left alive.

"We are Claira!" someone shouted, and all the soldiers who had heard it echoed, "We are Claira!" The call-and-response continued: "We are strong! We are brave! We cannot be defeated!"

Despite her pain, Denavi smiled. We are Claira. We cannot be defeated. Saber Company would return home to glory and honor, the only goals of a true Clairan.

"Springtime is one of my favorite seasons," Ezalen Skywing said as he strolled through the Reading Square in the Introvertian capital city of Tranquility. "Look! The cherry and dogwood trees are in full bloom now. Do you smell the flowers? And over there, that's an osprey nest. Look how huge it is. Give it about six weeks and you'll see the hatchlings poke their heads over the sides." Eza took a huge breath, enjoying the evening breeze as the sun set behind them and turned the sky purple.

"Everyone has an extra bounce in their step these days. I wonder if that's why they call it spring."

"You talk too much," teased Cammie Ravenwood.

The two of them stared at each other and then burst out laughing. Cammie was from Exclaimovia, a nation that Eza had once known as "The Kingdom of People Yelling and Having No Concept of Personal Space," and she babbled Eza's ear off every chance she got. "I was only talking because you hate silence," he said with a huge smile.

"I know. You're really kind to me." Her dark hair brushed against her shoulder blades as she walked; she'd taken to wearing it down, in Introvertian style.

"I try." Eza thought for a second. "You know, summer is one of my favorite seasons, too. I love those long, warm nights when I can stay up reading until my eyes just drop shut. I like autumn, too, the change of colors and the smell of the cool evenings. Winter isn't my favorite, but wow, curling up in front of the fire with a book in your hands is one of the best things in life, isn't it?"

"They're going to kick you out of the Reading Square if you keep rambling."

"Fine. I'll be silent the rest of the way to the Academy, then."

Cammie's eyes got huge – one of them brown, one

blue. "No, no...you don't have to."

Eza chuckled to himself. It had been fun watching Cammie adapt to life in Introvertia. The week before, Cammie and Eza had made a daring trip to Exclaimovia to steal back some magical dragons that the Exclaimovians had taken from Introvertia. Somehow they'd been successful. But Cammie hadn't been able to go back to Exclaimovia; she'd been banished for doing the right thing, and she was no longer welcome in her home country.

Graciously, King Jazan and Queen Annaya of Introvertia had allowed Cammie the opportunity to enroll in the Dragon Academy with Eza, despite the fact that she hadn't passed the Year of Silence (and never would – she'd have a hard time passing the "Five Minutes of Silence," Eza thought) and would likely never have a mental link with a dragon the way the other students could. What other choice was there, though? Cammie had been exiled from her home for helping Introvertia; the *least* Eza's people could do was give her whatever she wanted as a reward.

The other interesting wrinkle was that both Cammie and Eza had returned with magical ability. Officially, Introvertia was a non-magical society. Eight hundred years before, tired of people using magic the wrong way, Introvertia had given up the practice entirely. Most spellcasters had either left the kingdom or had been forced to keep their abilities secret. Yet Eza had been trained in the ancient school of Artomancy, and Cammie was born with elemental magic ability. They'd told the king and queen about their magic, but had been instructed to keep it hidden from everyone else.

"You got quiet," Cammie said, poking him in the side.

Eza danced away from her finger. "Sorry. I was just thinking about you being here and how much fun it's been. I know it's been hard for you to be away from your family, because you love them a lot."

Cammie's face clouded over. "I just hate that they all think I'm a traitor. Not my parents and brother, because they know the truth, but my aunts and uncles and cousins and grandparents, and all the rest of Exclaimovia. The dragon theft was so secret that the government couldn't tell people that I'd been kicked out for helping to steal them back, so it told everyone a lie and now they all believe it."

"I hope we get the chance to set the record straight one day."

"Me too. But I have to say, I'm enjoying Introvertia more every day. I know there are some people who think I'm too much..."

"You are."

Cammie lunged for Eza's sides again, but he escaped, laughing at his own joke. "But, you know, the best kind of too much," he added.

Cammie giggled, adjusting her glasses. "Thank you. We keep rubbing off on each other, you know. I accept compliments from you, at least every once in a while, and you tease people."

Eza considered that. "When I compliment people, they smile. When I tease the right people in the right way, they smile too. You just did. So...that's kind of the same thing, right?"

"Hmm. Fair point."

They had exited the Reading Square by now, turning left to head toward Carnazon Fortress, the citadel on the northeast side of Tranquility that housed the Dragon Academy. Tonight was Tuesday, and all the students had been told in class that there would be a major announcement on Wednesday morning. Hardly anything productive had gotten done in Writing or Dragon Care class that afternoon as the students speculated about what the announcement might be. Eza neared the south gate of the fortress, surprised by the sound of – well, not a commotion, but the closest thing to it that a group of Introvertians could ever produce: a game of ringball in the main courtyard.

It was every company for itself with three balls in

play, Eza could see. Victory, Harmony, Excellence, and Sun were the four companies in which an Academy student could be placed depending on his or her personality and what he or she wanted to be upon graduation. Eza poked his head through the open gateway; the score was usually chalked onto the far wall, and sure enough, there it was. "Sun is winning," he told Cammie in surprise. "I've never seen that before."

"Good for them!"

The two of them edged their way into the courtyard, then sprinted as fast as they could for the doorway to their left, which led to a staircase and the Harmony lounge on the second floor of the fortress. The sounds of the ringball game were muffled but still audible in the lounge between the boys' and girls' dorms, with its huge windows that overlooked the courtyard. In centuries past, when Introvertia had fought wars against the distant kingdoms of Telravia and Claira and even Esteria and Exclaimovia, these dormitories had been barracks for the soldiers who defended Carnazon from attackers. The fortress had been the site of twelve major battles, and it had never been conquered. Just being in the same place where those ancient heroes had once stood filled Eza with pride.

"I guess I should probably do my Dragon Care homework," Cammie said. "I, uh...didn't get much done in class today."

"None of us did," Eza said with a smile. "Do you need any help?"

"I'd love some. I missed the first two years of the class, after all, and I can't talk to dragons like the rest of you can, so..."

"Grab some paper and light a candle, then!"

TWO

About forty Harmony third-year girls shared a dorm with Cammie, their beds lined up along the left-hand side. The windows on the outer wall overlooked the courtyard – and faced east, which meant the dorm got bright *very* early in the morning. As soon as the sun began peeking over the Impassable Mountains, some of the girls were already up, mostly the ones who were studying to be Rangers, frontier scouts. That was also what Eza wanted to be, and he'd told Cammie before how he'd had to train himself to be a light sleeper, because it would be really bad for a Ranger to be surprised by an enemy or a wild beast. Apparently these girls took that very seriously, because they were fully dressed before the mess hall was even serving breakfast.

Cammie wanted to go back to sleep, but now that she was awake, her head was clogged with thoughts about the big announcement, and there was no chance she'd be able to relax again. With a dramatic sigh, she shoved herself over the side of the bed, stretched her arms and legs and fingers and toes, and started her morning routine. The Introvertian girls had an incredible way of getting ready in ten minutes; some kept their hair short so they didn't have to do anything but brush it, and some threw it into a ponytail or something else easy to manage. Cammie liked to take time braiding hers, even if it was only a small part on one side. She had fun doing it differently every day, or changing her clothes at lunchtime, or dyeing her boots purple and then red and then pink. She knew the Introvertians didn't understand that side of her, but she wasn't trying to please them. She was Cammie Ravenwood, and that was who she wanted to be.

"What do you think the announcement is?" she asked Anneka Azoana, who wanted to work in the government helping to manage the dragon program.

"You asked me that fourteen times yesterday," Anneka said flatly.

"Yeah, well...you may have thought of something."

"I thought of the fact that we're all going to know in about an hour and a half after breakfast, so it's kind of pointless to speculate now, isn't it?"

"Okay," Cammie said, a little wounded. This kind of thing happened to her dozens of times a day. Most Introvertians were generous and polite, and quite a few of Cammie's classmates had even gone out of their way to show her kindness. But more than a few of them were...not even *shy,* but actually aloof, deliberately distant. They were within their rights to feel that way, Cammie knew. This was *their* school and this was *their* country. She was the interloper. But it still hurt.

The only people who never made her feel out of place were Eza and his friend Shanna Cazaran, who was a few feet away from Cammie getting ready. If Cammie didn't know better, she'd swear Eza and Shanna were siblings; they looked so much alike except that Shanna's hair was darker, and they spoke and acted like as if they shared a brain. Shanna must have felt Cammie's eyes on the back of her head, because she looked over at Cammie and smiled. "Can I help you with your hair?" Shanna asked.

"Thank you," Cammie said, "but I'm going to leave it simple today."

Shanna tilted her head, the same way Eza always did. "I like when you braid it."

A smile found its way to Cammie's face, and she beamed with pride. It was nice to be appreciated. "Okay. I'll braid it."

Eza was standing in front of the windows in the lounge, his hands behind his back, waiting for Cammie when she finally arrived. "How long have you been there?" she asked.

Eza checked the sun. "A couple of hours."

"Wow! What time did you wake up?"

"Razan sneezed at about four, and I've been awake since. I made the mistake of thinking about that big announcement and couldn't get back to sleep."

Cammie giggled. "What do you think it is?" She'd asked Eza that question *at least* fourteen times, but unlike Anneka, he'd made a game out of it and given a different answer every time.

"I think they're going to outlaw small talk."

Cammie let her jaw fall open in pretend shock. "You'll be arrested for sure!"

"I'll be arrested at the same time as you!" Eza laughed. "Maybe they'll give us cells next to each other."

Shanna joined them and the trio went down to breakfast together. Razan Enara, Eza's other close friend, had apparently overslept after waking up to sneeze, because he wasn't in the lounge by the time they left. Cammie scarfed down her steak, eggs, and fruit juice, making sure no one was looking when she sprinkled the whole plate with the secret jar of Exclaimovian spices that she kept in her backpack. Cammie was pretty sure some of the other students were staring in her direction, at the Exclaimovian and the two Introvertians laughing together perhaps a little too loudly, but she didn't care. Before she knew it, the clock was showing only fifteen minutes until the announcement was due to take place, and the mess hall began to clear out.

The main courtyard was the only part of the Academy large enough to accommodate all sixteen hundred students, and a podium had been set up by the southern gate. Students were pouring from the mess hall, and out of the western staircase that led down from the Harmony and Victory dorms, as well as down the eastern staircase from the Excellence and Sun dorms. Several minutes before nine – Introvertians were punctual, Cammie had discovered, whereas Exclaimovians had no problem being half an hour late if they ran into someone interesting on the way – the courtyard was full, and at nine o'clock on the nose a woman rose to the podium. Cammie hadn't met her, but had seen her at a distance a number of times, and recognized her as General Leazan, the director of the Dragon Academy. The general was tall, about forty, with a sharp nose and steel-gray hair, and as soon as she placed both hands on the podium and straightened her back, the whole courtyard grew silent.

"Good morning, students and faculty," General Leazan began. "A week and a half ago, two of our very own students, Ezalen Skywing and Cammaina Ravenwood, engaged in an act of daring bravery. At great danger to themselves, they infiltrated Exclaimovia and liberated a number of dragons which the Exclaimovians had stolen from us and were attempting to train into their own dragon army."

Polite applause broke out, and Eza and Cammie waved to the students around them.

General Leazan held up her hand and silence fell again. "Those of you who have received a dragon in the past ten days have these two students to thank. However, Cadet Skywing and Cadet Ravenwood did not merely return with dragons. They returned with valuable knowledge as well. We all know that Introvertian dragons are not as large as the stories say they once were. Their magical ability, their fire-breathing, is...shall we say, unimpressive. Now we know the reason why. Dragons are fed by magical energy inside their companion. When Introvertia made the decision eight hundred years ago to banish magic from our society, our dragons began to starve – not physically, but magically, one might say. Their growth was stunted."

The general surveyed her students. "King Jazan and Queen Annaya have been faced with a very difficult decision. Introvertia's choice to reject magic was a careful and deliberate one, all those centuries in the past. Our kingdom has not been ravaged by an evil sorcerer since. However, now that we know our dragons require magic in order to thrive, we stand at a crossroads. We cannot call ourselves dragon-companions if we are withholding something they need. We must either do what's right for our dragons, or else release them all."

Cammie's eyes were wide and she was breathing hard. She glanced at Eza; his shoulders were tense and he was squinting with concentration. How was this going to end?

"So," General Leazan concluded, "King Jazan and Queen Annaya have chosen to permit the reintroduction of magic into Introvertian society, starting with you, the Dragon Academy students. Beginning today, each of you will have a magic class added to your normal course load. Most of you will spend your first class selecting a school of magic to study, after which you will begin intensive training. Again, I must remind you that this is for the good of your dragon. You must be proficient in magic in order for your dragon to grow to its full size and strength. Please take this task seriously. Thank you."

The courtyard erupted in applause and cheers and students chattering excitedly. Cammie grabbed Eza by the shoulders. "Magic class!" she shouted gleefully.

"I can't believe it," he said in delight. "This is the best news we could have gotten! We don't have to hide anymore!"

All around Cammie and Eza, students leaped for joy. Some laughed and some even cried from happiness. Cammie couldn't blame them; she knew what a thrill it was when magical energy poured through her body, and it was worth getting excited about. She couldn't help but smile at the noise and the joy that surrounded her.

The first magic class had been scheduled for after

lunch, though, and Cammie couldn't help but feel sorry for Professor Ozara and his History class, and Professor Grenalla and her Survivalship class, both of which were supposed to happen in the morning. There was *no way* the students would be able to focus on anything if they knew they were *about to start learning magic* in a few hours.

Professor Ozara, however, had a trick up his sleeve. His lecture was about the history of magic in Introvertia, and he kept reminding the students that if they didn't learn from the past, they would make the same mistakes as the ancient Introvertians did, and magic would end up banned again. That got everyone's attention, and Cammie had never seen the class so focused on taking notes. Even Eza, who had read *Legends of the Artomancers* and already knew nearly everything the professor was saying, listened intently and dutifully wrote down the few tidbits he hadn't heard before.

It was harder for Professor Grenalla to connect magic to survivalship. The class itself dealt with all the things Eza and Shanna would need to know as Rangers: how to find a path through mountains, how to identify which plants were food and which were poisonous, how to find water based on what vegetation was nearby, and all of that. It wasn't Cammie's favorite class; she hadn't spent a lot of time outside when she was younger, preferring to excel in her classwork instead, but she had learned a lot that would be useful if she ever suddenly decided to take up camping. Now that most of the students had dragons to take care of, Professor Grenalla had spent the last few class sessions on how a Ranger could use his or her dragon to help look for food or water, or to keep an eye out for enemies. This made it even harder for Cammie to pay attention; she knew there was almost no chance she would ever have a dragon of her own, and she tried to pay attention just in case it somehow became possible. Some days she was successful and some days she wasn't. Today was a "wasn't."

After lunch the students were gathered into the main courtyard once again, with General Leazan near the podium and another man that Cammie didn't recognize standing next to her. "Who's that guy?" she asked Eza.

"I don't think I've seen him before."

But Cammie didn't have to wait long. General Leazan took the stage, and unlike in the morning, when the buzz of anticipation had calmed almost immediately, it took the students quite a while to settle down. They were just minutes from one of the most exciting things that would ever happen to them, after all. General Leazan smiled patiently; she was no-nonsense and a stickler for rules, but Cammie could tell from her face that she understood what the students were feeling. Eventually the courtyard was quiet enough for her voice to be heard, so she mounted the podium.

"Good afternoon, students and faculty. The moment you've been waiting for has arrived." The general smiled even more widely now; Cammie could tell she was almost as invigorated as the students. "I'm pleased to introduce to you the director of Carnazon's Magical Studies department. Please welcome Colonel Aric Ennazar."

Raucous applause erupted from the students, but Eza frowned in confusion. "Colonel?" she saw him mouth to himself. Immediately she saw what he was wondering. If Colonel Ennazar was a spellcaster himself, he'd made it awfully high up in the military without anyone finding out – or maybe they had found out, but he'd managed to keep a tight lid on it. Maybe he couldn't actually use magic himself and was just an overseer the army had appointed. Cammie had lots of questions, and she loved finding out answers to questions.

Colonel Ennazar took the podium, smiling and waving to the assembly. He looked about thirty years old, which was awfully young to have made such a high rank already. His hair was light brown, just a bit darker than Eza's, and came to just below his chin. "I understand you want to learn magic!" he shouted theatrically, raising both hands in the air.

The students' roar reverberated off the stone walls of the courtyard and nearly deafened Cammie. Warm memories washed over her, and for a moment she was back in the Shouting Square in Exclaimovia's capital city of Pride. Her smile faded, and Eza touched her arm. "Are you okay?" he asked.

"Just missing home."

There was no time for her to explain more, because Colonel Ennazar raised his hand and launched a ball of fire into the air. The ball rose into the air above Carnazon, then quickly grew until it was fifty feet around. Then it began falling, falling –

Ennazar extended his arms again, shouting triumphantly, and water cannoned out of him, meeting the fireball and making a giant cascade of steam that caught the afternoon sun and turned into a rainbow. In moments the flame was gone and only a light mist sprinkled the students in the center of the courtyard. Cammie clapped along with all the other students; she had always loved being dramatic and showing off, so Ennazar's spectacle resonated with her.

Eza elbowed her in the ribs. "He's an elemental mage like you."

Cammie hadn't even thought of that, and her eyes got huge. "He'll be training me?"

Eza laughed. "Just imagine how good you'll be when

he gets done."

"Whoa..."

A few other spellcasters had approached the podium by this time, and the students were treated to a demonstration of Artomancy, physical magic, and defensive magic. Along with elemental, those were the four schools of magic, and all the students would select the one they most wanted to learn. Eza and Cammie were already locked to their schools; Gar the Artomancer, who had trained Eza in the Artomancers' Prismatic City, had explained that once a person began learning one school, the others "closed themselves off," in his words. The choice was permanent.

General Leazan spoke one final time, informing the students that first-years would have their magic class on Mondays (a great moan of disappointment went up once they realized they would have to wait five whole days for their first class), second-years on Tuesdays (an even greater moan for their six-day wait), third-years on Wednesdays ("Does that mean today or next Wednesday?" they asked each other anxiously), fourth-years on Thursdays starting tomorrow, and fifth-years on Fridays. After that, the students were dismissed – including the third-years to their magic classes. "Elemental magic will be here in the courtyard, so if you wish to be elemental, stay where you are. Artomancy is in the east side function room, where the quarterly formal dances are held. Defensive magic is atop the west side wall. Physical magic, you'll follow Professor Kenzana outside the city walls. Dismissed!"

This would be the only class Cammie didn't have with Eza. She was very excited to learn more about elemental magic – especially from Colonel Ennazar – but she was also very aware that this would be the only class where she didn't have any friends. Eza was in Artomancy, and it looked like Shanna had chosen physical magic. Elemental appeared to have the largest crowd; out of the three hundred or so third-years in the school, nearly a hundred and twenty had remained in the courtyard. Many of them Cammie recognized from Victory Company, which made sense; elemental magic was attack-minded and strong, and most of Victory wanted to be front-line combat fighters. Ah – there was someone she recognized: Eza's friend Razan. Eza had described the dark-haired boy as "quieter and more serious than Shanna and me," and Razan had already been the wobbly third wheel in that relationship even before Cammie came and made everything even louder. Razan still hung out with them, but it seemed to Cammie that was only because he didn't have very many other friends.

"Hey, Razan," she greeted him.

"Oh, hey, Cammie," he said, his face brightening. "You want to be an elemental mage?"

"I already am," she said.

Razan frowned. "What?"

Cammie held out her hand and summoned a small fireball into her palm, turning it around and then poofing it into the afternoon sun. "Eza and I have already learned magic. The king and queen knew, and they told us to keep it a secret. But now that everyone is learning, I guess we don't have to."

Razan didn't seem to know what to make of this. "Eza kept secrets from me?"

"He didn't want to," Cammie said, suddenly wondering if she'd said the wrong thing. "But King Jazan and Queen Annaya ordered him to."

"Okay."

She could tell Razan wasn't happy about that, but she wasn't going to let him dampen the mood. It was time for her to let her magic out, and to become the best spellcaster she could possibly be.

Aric Ennazar stepped to the podium and cleared his throat, and Cammie couldn't stop a huge smile from leaping to her face.

THREE

The courtyard hadn't emptied yet.

It was five o'clock in the afternoon. Magic class had ended several hours ago, but the elemental students were still there, working over and over and over at what Colonel Ennazar had taught them. His first lecture had dealt with concentration and focus, and it had gone *very* well. Cammie knew she shouldn't have been surprised that students who had recently spent a year in total silence would be good at clearing their minds and single-mindedly fixating on an idea. By the end of that first hour, most of the students could make a poof of fire in their palms, and a few of the really advanced ones could make tiny sparks of lightning that tickled like crazy when they hit someone. Cammie had paid careful attention to the lecture, even though it was material she'd already taught herself back in Exclaimovia, but she hadn't shown off any magic of her own yet. Razan's earlier reaction had bothered her. She didn't want anyone else to know that the Exclaimovian, who some students already didn't like, had been hiding magic from them too.

Cammie heard two familiar voices coming toward her and turned to see Eza and Shanna picking their way across the crowded courtyard. She hadn't realized how tense her shoulders were until they relaxed at the sight of her friends. "Hey, Eza!" she shouted with a smile and a wave.

She hadn't noticed Anneka Azoana standing within arm's reach, and the Introvertian girl leaned away, holding her ear. "Don't shout," Anneka admonished.

"People have been shouting for joy all day long," protested Cammie. "Use your head."

"You didn't need to shout at Ezalen anyway. He's right there; he'll be over here in less than a minute."

"I'm sorry if all your friends are so boring that you don't celebrate when you see them coming," Cammie said, her inner actress coming out as she faked an expression of intense sympathy. "Perhaps you should make more interesting friends as soon as possible."

"That's the problem with you Exclaimovians," Anneka said, throwing up her hands. "You all think you're so much better than us."

"How many Exclaimovians have you even met?" Cammie snapped, her hand going to her waist.

Eza must have seen the gesture from across the courtyard, because he seemed to hurry up, but Cammie held up her hand. She was going to fight this one herself.

"One is enough."

Cammie's temper was getting away from her, and she

threw her hands into the air in frustration. When she did, huge puffs of flame launched out from her palms, harmlessly into the sky. *Oh, no...*

"What was THAT?" Anneka asked in shock. "You didn't learn magic that strong just today."

"Oh, you didn't know?" Razan said, shouldering in on the conversation. "She's had magical ability all along and has been keeping it secret from us."

"Is that true?" Anneka asked in disbelief.

"It's true, alright," Cammie agreed. If they wanted a show, she was going to give them a show. Eza had made it to her side by this point, and Cammie blasted off the biggest, most powerful fireball she could summon without exhausting herself, launching it off to the northeast.

That got the attention of nearly everyone in the courtyard, and the excited murmurs fell silent as all eyes searched for the source of the magical outburst. "Eza and I came back from Exclaimovia with magic," Cammie said, loudly enough that everyone could hear. "We found out about dragons feeding on magical energy, and we're the reason the king and queen decided to bring back magic." She raised her voice louder than she had since she was last in the Shouting Square. "SO I'D JUST LIKE TO SAY YOU'RE ALL WELCOME!"

She could see dozens of people cringe when she did,

but she was past the point of caring. "I don't care *what* you did," spat Anneka. "You're loud, and you're rude. You're an embarrassment to the Academy and I don't know why they ever took you in."

"Because –"

"You should hear what people say about you behind your back if you think *we're* being rude," Razan goaded. "At least we have the courage to say it straight to your face."

It was Shanna, of all people, who shoved herself between Cammie and the other two Introvertians. *"WHAT IS WRONG WITH YOU TWO?"* Shanna screamed at the top of her voice, facing Anneka and Razan. Cammie nearly smiled; having been trained for the stage, she couldn't help but admire the strength with which Shanna projected her voice, considering Cammie had never heard her make any noise louder than a sneeze.

If it were possible to die of surprise, someone would have been dragging Razan and Anneka's corpses out of the courtyard by their ankles. *"She gave up EVERYTHING to help us!"* Shanna continued, her hands in the air. "You have your very own *DRAGON* at your house *RIGHT NOW* because she went against her people to do the right thing. She got kicked out of her home for it and lost her family. And we do the right thing and give her a new home, but all you two *IDIOTS* can do is harass her!" She stared down Razan and Anneka, who were glancing around as if trying to find someone who would back them up. Shock was all they saw; Cammie had never heard one Introvertian yell at another, and judging from the faces of the people nearby, none of them had either.

"THAT'S NOT WHO WE ARE, PEOPLE!" Shanna finished, somehow even louder than before. "WE'RE BETTER THAN THAT! WE ARE KIND, WE ARE LOVING, AND WE NEED TO ACT LIKE IT!"

"Now you're yelling too!" Anneka accused. "You've been spending too much time around her. Her and Eza; he's the problem too..."

"If you're really more upset at me for yelling than at yourself for being rude to a girl who's *only ever been kind to you,* then you need to –"

Professor Grenalla had been making her way across the crowded courtyard as well, and reached Shanna before she could finish the sentence. "Is everything alright here?" the teacher asked.

"Dandy," said Shanna. "Anneka and Razan were just leaving."

Anneka walked past Cammie, bumping shoulders with her on the way and avoiding eye contact. Razan disappeared into the crowd. Cammie touched Shanna on the arm. "Thanks."

Shanna grinned. "I meant it."

"We love you, Cammie!" someone shouted, and dozens or hundreds of voices echoed, "We love you, Cammie!"

The smile on her face was so huge it almost hurt. Cammie waved at everyone. "You're the best!"

Eza leaned in close and said, "Maybe it would be best if we left for a while, anyway. I've got a bunch of food in my backpack. Want to join me for a picnic outside the city gates?"

"That sounds wonderful."

The sun was just barely peeking over the western skyline of Tranquility as Eza led Cammie out the gates and to a clearing about a hundred yards off the main road. A few minutes later, a silhouette appeared in the sky, growing closer and closer before settling down next to Eza with a whoosh of wings. It was his dragon, Aleiza; he'd used his mind link to summon her from his house. Most Academy students who lived nearby left their dragons at home during the week, and called on them with the mind link when one of their classes required some hands-on-dragon experience. For the students who lived too far away, there was a dragon-stable across the street from Carnazon. Eza wished they could all keep their dragons in the barracks with them, but the dorm rooms were crowded enough as it was, and besides, the dragons would be bored with nothing to do all day. At least Aleiza could fly around when she wasn't with Eza.

But he still needed to spend time with her as much as he could so that she could grow off his magical energy, just like General Leazan had described. Eza was still a bit fuzzy on how all that worked, if they had to be touching each other or if just being close was okay, but Aleiza had grown another foot since she'd first met Eza, so obviously something was going right.

Eza gave Cammie some of the food out of his pack, and then passed her a glass jar. "Here," he said. "Try this."

The light was almost gone, stars beginning to peek out in the sky above them, and Cammie couldn't see the bottle clearly. "I've seen you using those Exclaimovian spices on your food," he said.

"I thought I was hiding them well..."

"Yeah, well, Rangers notice things."

"You didn't notice this," Cammie said, poking him under his ribs.

Eza laughed and rolled away, and Aleiza jerked up at the sound. The dragon had never grown to like sudden noises. "Not fair," Eza protested. "It's dark out. Anyway, I went and asked somebody what seasonings –"

"It was Mr. Cappel, wasn't it?"

"I asked *somebody...*"

"Mr. Cappel."

"Fine, I asked Mr. Cappel if he knew what seasonings Exclaimovians liked to use, and don't ask me how, but he had an Exclaimovian cookbook on hand."

"There's something weird about that guy," Cammie blurted. "When he first met me he made it sound like he'd known Exclaimovians before. Now you're saying he has one of our cookbooks? Why would he need something like that?"

"Mr. Cappel is a unique individual," Eza said, choosing his words carefully. "I love him a lot, but he's not what you might call normal."

"Normal just means average, and who wants to be average?"

"Not me," Eza said with a smile.

"Not me," echoed Cammie.

"Anyway, you can imagine I couldn't get most of the plants I needed here in Tranquility. Some I was able to find outside the city, and some I substituted for the closest thing I could find. So here. Ezalen Skywing's unique, one-of-a-kind pretend-Exclaimovian spice blend." Even in the starlight Cammie could see he was proud of himself. "I tried some and it tasted like being shouted at by a room full of strangers, so I'm sure you'll love it."

That made Cammie laugh uncontrollably, and she popped open the jar to shake it on the meat and grilled vegetables. "It's...actually really good," she said in surprise.

"You doubted my foraging abilities?" Eza asked, pretending to be offended.

"No, just your palate." She stuffed another bite in her mouth and said, through the food, "It's wonderful, though. It tastes like home."

They ate together as the stars glittered above them, Eza tossing pieces of meat occasionally to Aleiza, who caught them out of the air and chomped a few times before swallowing them mostly whole. "When you're done," Eza said, "we should duel."

"Duel?" Cammie asked, rolling over onto her stomach and resting her chin on her hands. "I don't swordfight."

"Not swords. Magic."

"A magic duel?" Cammie's voice was full of excitement. "But...what if we hurt each other?"

"We'll hold back. Try not to hit Aleiza, though. Loser does the winner's laundry next week."

Cammie giggled. "There's Eza, always making everything a competition." She scarfed down the rest of her food and stood up. "I'm ready. Let's go."

They moved about twenty steps apart before turning

to face each other. The moon had just come over the Impassable Mountains, bathing the grassy field in a delicate white glow. Eza could clearly see Cammie standing, left foot forward and right foot back, knees bent in a ready position and her hands down at her waist. "On three," Eza said. "One, two, three!"

A weakly glowing fireball surged past Eza's head, and he shoulder-rolled to his left, whipping his hand as if painting while he did. The air between him and Cammie turned a brilliant cobalt blue, like the summer sky, and Eza closed his eyes. A sun appeared in the sky he'd drawn, lighting the whole area – or he assumed it did; he couldn't see it himself – and Cammie gave a shout of surprise. When Eza opened his eyes, the summer scene was gone and Cammie was staggering backward, reeling from the sudden bright light. He sprinted forward and tickled her ribs, making her squeal and flail around.

"I can't see you!" she shouted.

"Do you concede?"

"Never!"

"Never is a long time," he teased, still poking her.

Almost too late he saw the crackle of electrical energy in her palms, and he threw himself to the ground again as lightning spider-webbed into the place where his voice had just come from. "Clever," he said, backing away. "But I can do better."

Cammie looked as if her eyes were clearing, and she fixed her gaze on Eza. "Here comes a big one," she warned.

"Hit me."

Eza had never seen her try ice before, but a long beam of it erupted from her hands. He threw his own hands in front of him, furiously drawing, and a shimmering multicolored oval opened in the air at his fingertips – a rainbow door. An identical hole opened behind him, and the ice beam passed in the front one and out the back one, leaving Eza unscathed in the middle. The rainbow door was one of the most advanced spells he knew, and it could do one other thing – maybe –

Quickly he redrew the spell and the rear door moved, appearing just behind Cammie. Eza stepped through the door in front of him –

And suddenly he was on the other side of the field, with Cammie facing the other way directly in front of him. He reached out again and tickled her sides, and she screamed as she jumped away. But this time her response was immediate. The ground underneath Eza wobbled and he lost his footing; that was her earth magic. In the next moment a cannon of water blasted him off his feet and he tumbled to the ground, soaked through.

"Do you concede?" she taunted him.

"Never!"

"You there!" someone shouted on the far end of the clearing, and instantly Eza was back on his feet, shoulder to shoulder with Cammie and squinting into the darkness.

"Show yourself," Eza ordered.

Eight members of the Tranquility city guard stepped closer. "What's been happening here?" one of them demanded, but without anger.

"We're Dragon Academy students. We were practicing our magic."

"Ah." The guard had apparently heard of the day's announcement at Carnazon; it was probably impossible to be standing at the city gate all day long, right outside the courtyard, and not have heard what was going on. "We saw the lights and we wondered. Carry on."

They disappeared back toward the city, and Eza chuckled. "I guess that means it's a draw?"

"Who does the laundry, then?" An idea seemed to hit Cammie. "Since we both sort of won and sort of lost, how about we do each other's laundry?"

"You wear three or four outfits a day," objected Eza. "It'll take all weekend to do yours."

"And yet I manage." Cammie flipped her hair out to the side and put her hand on her hip. "Unless you're saying a girl can do something a boy can't do."

Cammie had prodded him perfectly, and they both knew it: she had made this into a competition. Eza bit the inside of his lip; there was *no way* he was going to let himself be baited into doing Cammie's laundry just because she had laid down a challenge. But he didn't know how else to respond; the word "no" just didn't seem to be in his head when it came to something like this.

"I'll take your deal, Cammaina Ravenwood," he said with a smile, extending his hand to shake hers. "This one time."

"Mmhmm," Cammie said, grinning mischievously. "Just this one time, I'm sure."

They sat down next to each other on the grass and Aleiza lumbered over. Eza sensed excitement and curiosity coming off her; she had clearly enjoyed watching the duel and was now soaking up whatever magical energy was still wafting off Eza and Cammie. "That was really nice, what Shanna did back there," Cammie told Eza, looking up at the stars.

"Shanna's great. She said what a lot of us were thinking." Eza smirked again. "Maybe a little more loudly than the rest of us would have, but I have no doubt she made an impression." He looked over at Cammie, the frame of her glasses silhouetted against the sky. "I haven't told you this, but I really admire you."

"Me?" Cammie asked, bewildered. Eza knew how Cammie felt about compliments. She'd done a lot better with accepting them lately, but she still came from a culture where compliments were used to flatter and manipulate people. *I admire you* was a lot to dump on her, and Eza hoped he hadn't gone overboard.

"Yeah, you. What Shanna said was the truth. You sacrificed everything to help us, and you came here to a kingdom you barely knew, no family, only one friend..."

"A really good one, though."

"A really good one who doesn't mind at all when you interrupt," Eza teased.

"I know you don't," Cammie said, pretending to be oblivious.

"And you've just handled it all so gracefully," Eza continued. "With such incredible strength. You've been patient with the people who've been rude to you. You're just...really amazing."

"Okay, just because I let you compliment me sometimes doesn't mean I can handle an entire wagonload at once."

"You'll live," Eza laughed.

But Cammie fidgeted. "Do you think there are a lot of others who agree with Razan and Anneka? Who secretly don't want me here?"

"Probably a good number of them, yeah."

He could feel Cammie grimace next to him. "I forgot you don't lie."

"I respect you too much to lie to you. You have to keep in mind that Introvertians don't like conflict. We like to be left alone to do things our own way. All we've ever wanted since we first became an independent kingdom is to mind our own business. So people like Razan, they don't dislike *you*. They dislike what you represent, which is the outside world intruding into their comfort zone."

"I am *definitely* outside their comfort zone," Cammie agreed. "I suppose I've never really said thank you. You accept me as I am. I appreciate that."

"But I didn't always," pointed out Eza. "We fought *a whole lot* at first, until we got to know each other. That's why I'm not worried about Razan and Anneka. They'll come around, Cammie. Some already have come around; you heard how many people said they love you. Some will come around soon, and some will take a while. I guess there's a chance that some might never, but that's out of your hands. You can't control whether other people choose to like you or not."

"I'm glad you choose to."

Eza smiled. "Me too."

Cammie leaned her head sideways so it rested on his shoulder, and together they watched the stars shimmering.

FOUR

It was lunchtime on Thursday when Cammie and Eza, eating with Shanna like usual (Razan had chosen a new seat at a distant table), noticed someone unexpected enter the mess hall. It wasn't uncommon for one of the king's messengers came to Carnazon, but the message in question was usually for General Leazan or one of the professors or someone else in authority. For a messenger to visit the mess hall, where only the students ate, was something Eza hadn't seen before. Even more surprisingly, the messenger asked an inaudible question to a Harmony student near the door, and the student pointed directly at Eza.

He stood as the messenger approached, unsure what was about to happen. "Ezalen Skywing?" the messenger asked.

Eza saluted, his right fist touching his opposite shoulder. "At the king's service."

"You are instructed to report to the palace at your earliest convenience, along with Cammaina Ravenwood." He handed Eza a piece of paper with these instructions on it.

Cammie, who was sitting right next to Eza, tensed at the mention of her name.

"Whatever the kingdom requires," Eza said smoothly, hoping his nervousness didn't show through. As he sat back down, he looked at Cammie. "No, before you ask, I have no idea what that's about. We probably shouldn't keep the king and queen waiting, though."

His last meeting with King Jazan and Queen Annaya had been a jubilant one, immediately after he and Cammie had returned to Tranquility with several hundred Introvertian dragons circling above them. As far as Eza could tell, the royal family liked him, but he was anxious anyway. Maybe he had done something to upset them in the last week. Probably not, but that was the Ranger in him, always being prepared for the worst possible scenario.

Ten minutes later he and Cammie were exiting the south gate of Carnazon, Dragon Academy cloaks fastened around their necks. Cammie had changed into a more muted outfit, gray pants and a green shirt. It was a beautiful spring day in Tranquility, and Eza, in spite of his nervousness, couldn't help smiling at the people he made eye contact with. The two cadets headed south, toward Broad Avenue, where a right turn would take them toward the Reading Square and the palace.

A few blocks before Broad Avenue, an older woman stood by the street with a tray of cookies. "Would you like one?" she asked Eza and Cammie.

"How much would you like for them?" Eza asked.

"Oh, they're a gift!" the woman said happily. "It's a beautiful day in a beautiful city."

"Thank you," Eza told her, taking one for him and one for Cammie. "That's very kind of you."

"It's what we should all do for each other."

Eza munched his cookie as he and Cammie kept strolling. "That never happened in Exclaimovia," Cammie observed.

"It should happen more everywhere," Eza said. "But especially here. We really value kindness."

"*Most* of you do," answered Cammie, thinking of what had happened the night before.

"Yeah, well, I've told you Introvertians come in all types. We're supposed to value kindness, I should have said. We're supposed to be welcoming and polite. Not all of us get there."

"I'm glad you're there."

Eza smiled. "I'm glad you were patient with me when all I saw was a loud Exclaimovian."

"I'm glad you were patient with me when all I wanted was to yell at a quiet Introvertian."

"That's the way things are supposed to work, I think," Eza said, making their right turn onto Broad Avenue. "People being patient with each other."

"You're feeling sentimental today."

Eza laughed. "Just rambling because I'm nervous."

"Oh." Cammie thought about that. "I ramble because it's fun to ramble."

Broad Avenue spread out before them, sixty feet wide and lined on both sides with homes and shops. The buildings had been made from local wood and gray stone, built to look as if the city were an extension of the forest which surrounded it. Just there on the left side was Cappel's Bookstore. Eza was planning to stop by on his way back from the palace to thank Mr. Cappel for his help in putting those seasonings together for Cammie, and he knew Cammie wouldn't mind browsing the books.

Some of the people who walked past Eza were looking around, daydreaming or thinking about other things. Some of them, though, looked at Eza as they passed, and Introvertian custom encouraged people who made eye contact to say something kind to each other. "Those are nice boots!" Eza said to the first man who came his way.

"Thanks! You two are Dragon Academy students? Wow, that's really impressive!"

"Thanks!" He looked over at Cammie. "Sorry. I know this isn't your favorite part, but I like it."

She smiled. "I can handle compliments from you, most of the time. I'm still working on taking them from strangers."

Footsteps were coming up behind Cammie and Eza now, and a younger girl, about nine years old, skipped past them. "Hi!" Eza greeted her. "Do you need any help getting where you're going?"

"Nope!" the girl said. "I'm strong and capable!"

"Yes, you are," Eza agreed with a huge smile.

"Thank you for being kind!" the girl sang over her shoulder as she skipped ahead.

A giant goofy grin was on Cammie's face. "That was so adorable," she said, clapping her hands.

"That's supposed to be normal," Eza told her. "The whole point of telling people nice things is so they come to believe it, without having to be told. Can you imagine a whole society where people believe the very best about themselves, where we all had the confidence of that girl? Where, if you're ever having a bad day or ever feeling a little sad, you have friends and strangers telling you all the things about yourself that are great?"

"When you say it like that..."

In a few more minutes (and a few more compliments) they had arrived in the Reading Square, one of Eza's favorite places but one that Cammie hadn't yet grown to like. Hundreds of Introvertians were scattered around the square, which was over three hundred feet on each side, and they were all silently reading. Cammie had explained that, for her, part of the fun of reading was to suddenly stop and show someone else whenever she found something neat or funny, but the people in the square didn't react well to her outbursts, so she and Eza typically read at his house or back at the Academy instead. It was an incredible day to be outside, though. The paved square was broken up every thirty feet or so by trees and flowers, and the crisp spring sunlight filtered down through the branches and leaves, making shadows that danced on the stone streets. It was like something out of a dream. Eza had gotten used to the sight, since he'd lived here his entire life, but every time they walked into the square he watched Cammie's face, to see the wonder overtake her all over again.

The royal palace was in the Reading Square, on the south end, backing up to the Rapidly Flowing River, which ran onward to Exclaimovia and there emptied into the Great Sea. Now the nervousness was catching up with Eza again, and he blew out a long breath. "Ready?" he asked.

"I don't know why you're on edge. They're probably going to give you a medal."

"Hey. I'm supposed to be the optimist."

Eza showed his message to the palace guards, who by this time probably recognized him on sight. He and Cammie were escorted into the throne room, where King

Jazan and Queen Annaya sat on their thrones at the far end of the room. Eza could tell as soon as he walked in that there was an air of tension. Something was not right. Out of one eye he spotted the row of chairs along the left side of the room, where half a dozen men sat – in Exclaimovian clothes. He stopped dead in the doorway.

"Cadet Skywing and Cadet Ravenwood," Queen Annaya greeted them. "Please, enter. Your presence has been requested by these honorable delegates from the Kingdom of Exclaimovia."

Besides Cammie, and maybe her family, Eza had never met anyone or anything from Exclaimovia that he would describe as "honorable." These were the people who interrupted each other while someone was telling a story so they could tell one of their own instead. They were the people who used compliments as manipulation, which was the reason Cammie still had a hard time receiving one. They had spent centuries violently oppressing Introvertians, demanding that the Introvertians in their society conform to the Exclaimovians' social customs, before the Introvertians had finally rebelled and fled to form their own kingdom. Mr. Cappel, whenever he'd told the story to Eza (as he'd done on multiple occasions), always ended that part of the tale with, "If you ever make an Introvertian mad enough to fight, you really messed up."

Cammie was hiding behind Eza, holding onto his shoulder so hard it was actually hurting him. "What do the king and queen require?" Eza said, trying not to wince in pain.

"We require our traitor back!" one of the Exclaimovians bellowed from the other side of the room.

But Eza didn't look, didn't dignify the man's outburst with a response. "What do the *king* and *queen* require?" he asked, softly and smoothly, keeping his eyes fixed on Queen Annaya, who had addressed him.

"I believe the delegate from Exclaimovia has just made his position known," she said, dark brown hair framing her brown eyes. She had been an actress in one of Tranquility's best theater troupes when she had caught King Jazan's eye, and their love story had captivated the whole kingdom for months until the royal wedding. Every one of her movements radiated grace and ease, the practiced movements of an accomplished dancer and actress. "Allow me to introduce Exclaimovia's Speaker for Diplomacy, Karrak Verakan."

"Cammaina Ravenwood is a traitor to our people, and she will return to stand trial," Verakan insisted, standing and taking a step toward Cammie. "She actively participated in a plot to undermine our government and to give aid and comfort to our enemies."

"Your enemies?" King Jazan asked mildly. He was taller than Queen Annaya, his hair also dark brown, though lighter than hers, and his eyes a bright hazel. "I was unaware, Speaker, that you numbered Introvertia among your enemies. Has there been a declaration of war that you neglected to bring me?"

"I meant our *historical* enemies, Your Highness, although there has been an extended period of peace between us recently."

King Jazan met Eza's gaze and raised one eyebrow in a look that said, *Can you believe this guy?* Eza nearly laughed in the middle of the throne room.

"The fact remains," Queen Annaya continued, stepping down and placing her hands on Cammie's shoulders, "that the full extent of Miss Ravenwood's activities were known to you at the time they were committed. Your government has already issued judgment in that case. You banished her from your kingdom. She requested asylum from us here in Introvertia, and we have granted that request. She is now under the protection of our kingdom. You cannot go back on your previous decision and insist that we hand her over to you. The law of asylum clearly dictates –"

"We may do anything we please with regard to one of our own citizens," Verakan said, cutting her off.

"I find two problems with that argument," King Jazan

said in the same mild, calm tone. "First, as you have banished her from your kingdom, she is no longer one of your citizens. In fact, she has taken an oath of allegiance to Introvertia. Second, and I am sure you are already well aware of this fact in your capacity as chief diplomat, Exclaimovia has never seen fit to sign a treaty of peace and recognition with Introvertia. Never in two thousand years, Speaker Verakan." His hazel eyes had turned hard. "As a result, we have no agreement to exchange prisoners. Since we are under no legal obligation to hand over *one of our own citizens* to you, we will decline."

"Refusing this demand is an act of war!" Verakan insisted, his eyes narrowed so he looked like a snake. "Are you prepared to risk war over a single sixteen-year-old girl?"

"Are *you*?" Queen Annaya asked. "We will risk war to protect any one of our citizens from injustice, and we will not bend to blackmail. The choice of whether to make war over Cadet Ravenwood is yours and yours alone. And may I remind you that, as our age of accountability is thirteen, Cadet Ravenwood is a full adult citizen of our society, with all the rights and privileges she deserves."

Karrak Verakan stood in place, looking back at the rest of his delegation as if out of ideas. Finally he faced the king and queen again. "I assure you this matter will be discussed with the highest seriousness within my government. I am sure that our new allies in Esteria and Claira will be most eager to learn of these developments."

"That sounds like a threat," King Jazan said, all mildness gone from his voice now.

Verakan spread his hands. "All statements of truth sound like threats to the one with a guilty conscience."

"You may tell your government," said the king, "that we will not be bullied. We have always been a people of peace. If you choose to regard it as an act of war when we give asylum to an Exclaimovian *whom you banished from your country,* that is your business. I cannot stop you from clothing yourself in dishonor. Now, are you making a declaration of war or not?"

"You will find out," said Verakan, sweeping out of the throne room with the remaining Exclaimovians behind him.

Cammie was shaking by now, and she gently pulled away from Queen Annaya to go stand next to Eza. He could hear her shallow, rapid breathing, and he could only imagine how stressed she must be. "You're with friends," he said softly.

Cammie just nodded.

"Let me see if I understand this," Queen Annaya said, turning to her husband. "Exclaimovia steals dragons from us, we steal them back, they banish the Exclaimovian who helped us, we take her in. Now they want her back so they can do as they please with her, and we won't give her back, and *that's* an act of war?"

"This whole thing reads like they were looking for an excuse to attack us," King Jazan said. "An alliance with Esteria and Claira was a curious move for them. Perhaps they just want to fight somebody over something and they don't care who or why."

Worry landed heavily on Queen Annaya's face. "How can we possibly defend against three nations at the same time? We haven't fought a war that large in...probably a thousand years. And the last time we did we had much stronger magic."

"It will take some time for the speaker to return home and then for an army to march to Tranquility, so if they're truly planning to attack, I would say we have about a week to craft our defense." King Jazan plopped back down onto his throne as if exhausted by the whole encounter. "Summon the chiefs of staff, please. We need a war council." He looked up at Cammie and Eza. "You two should probably remain here. Decisions may be made that impact you, and it would be best if you heard them for yourselves instead of having to be told."

They were shown to a small waiting chamber, where hot bread with butter and fresh fruit juice were waiting for them. Eza helped himself to the food; he was still anxious, but in his rush to leave the Academy for the palace he hadn't finished his lunch. Cammie hadn't stopped shaking, and as soon as Eza sat down next to her, she leaned against him. He set down his butter knife and put one hand on her opposite shoulder. Three weeks before, he'd tried to comfort her that way when she was upset the night before they'd left for Exclaimovia, and she'd jumped away and gotten upset at him. A lot had changed in the past three weeks.

Cammie's cheeks were wet, but Eza could tell she was stubbornly refusing to give in to the sobs that wanted to come out. "I hate when people see me cry," she said.

"Then I'll close my eyes."

That got a single laugh out of her, and the laugh gave way to tears, and then Cammie was crying. True to his word, Eza closed his eyes until Cammie started laugh-crying a few seconds later. "You don't have to look away, you goof," she told him.

"But I said –"

"I know what you said." She looked at Eza, wiping her eyes. "You don't think they're going to send me back to Exclaimovia, do you?"

"No chance. The king and queen will keep their word."

"But what if there's a war?"

"That's not up to you. That's up to Exclaimovia. I told you last night that you can't control other people and the choices they make, or how they react to the things you do. You can only control your own choices. And you've done the right thing."

"I hope so."

FIVE

It didn't take long for most of the top Introvertian generals to arrive from their posts around Tranquility. Eza didn't know many of the faces that he saw when he and Cammie reentered the throne room, but he did recognize General Leazan and Colonel Aric Ennazar off to one side. General Leazan was preoccupied, but Colonel Ennazar recognized Cammie and waved to her. She gave a half-smile and waved back.

King Jazan convened the war council and explained the meeting he'd just had with the Exclaimovians, including their alliance with the other two kingdoms and their threat of war. "We do not know whether Exclaimovia is truly going to attack," the king clarified. "Regardless, it is clear that we require a defensive plan, and quickly."

To Eza's shock, Colonel Ennazar stood, his hands behind his back, indicating that he wanted to speak. He was the lowest-ranked officer in the room and easily the youngest, and yet he had leaped to his feet without seeing if anyone else wanted to talk first. If the king were surprised, though, he didn't show it; he just nodded to Colonel Ennazar.

"If it please the council," the colonel began, "I am

Aric Ennazar, the recently appointed Director of Magical Studies at Carnazon. I am an elemental mage. Beginning when I was nine, my parents would take me to a camp on the northeast plains, where I would spend several weeks at a time sharpening my powers, and then I would return to Tranquility, keeping my gift secret and never using it. Many people encouraged me to flee Introvertia, to spend all my time working on magic and using it freely, but I could never bring myself to leave my home. I rose up through the ranks of the army, where a few of my commanding officers knew of my abilities and supported my decision to suppress them. When King Jazan and Queen Annaya reversed the edicts against magic use, and I was offered the opportunity to become an instructor of magic, it was one of the happiest days of my life."

He looked over the assembled generals, the king and queen, and then at last to Cammie and Eza. "I hope the council will not think me too forward for saying that magic may be the key to victory in this war. We have lost much of what we used to know, but not all." He looked over at Eza. "Cadet Skywing, this way, if you please."

Confused, Eza stepped forward. Colonel Ennazar motioned to the ground. "Can you create for us a map of the five kingdoms?"

Eza knew what the colonel was asking, so he looked

up, then bent down, sketching with his fingers on the ground. The map he was drawing on the ground appeared in midair, outlined in black, for the whole council to see, filling in as Eza labeled Introvertia in the southwest, Telravia just above it, Claira to the east of Telravia, Esteria east of that, and Exclaimovia directly south of Esteria. The Impassable Mountains and Very Large Forest between Introvertia and Exclaimovia were the last things he drew, and then he stepped back, looking at his handiwork.

"Cadet Skywing has been excelling in both History and Artomancy," Colonel Ennazar said approvingly. He then moved his own fingers, and thin filaments of fire connected dozens of different points on the map, the lines criscrossing and overlapping in places. "These are nexus lines, which represent currents of magical energy, so to speak," the colonel said. "The places where two or more lines cross are called nexus nodes. The more lines that cross in a particular place, the stronger the node they form. Those of you who are adept in magical history will notice the Prismatic City, home of the Artomancers, off to the east near Exclaimovia. Examine it closely and you'll see that the city is built on the intersection of five nexus lines. It is the single most powerful magical locations in the known world, the only five-line nexus node in existence, which is the reason it is widely believed to be unconquerable. Some of you are no doubt aware that Cadet Skywing, on his recent journey to Exclaimovia, stopped by the Prismatic City and received six 'terms' worth of Artomancy instruction in the space of thirty hours. Such accelerated learning, and the heightened power that comes along with it, is only possible at such a nexus node."

Heads were nodding around the room. "Some of you have also seen the wild dragon that Cadet Skywing collected," Colonel Ennazar added, "and wondered why it was nearly two feet taller than the typical domestic Introvertian dragon. Cadet, would you show the council where you bonded with that dragon?"

It was easy for Eza to find the place; three magical lines intersected right on it. He pointed, getting his finger as close to the air-map as he could without being burned by Ennazar's fire filaments.

"The dragon spent its entire life on a nexus node, being nourished by the latent magical energy." Colonel Ennazar looked up once more. "I hope I've convinced the council of the importance of these nodes. You will observe that a small number of them are found within Introvertia itself, while a number of more powerful ones can be found to the northeast. If we want our soldiers to be ready for magical warfare within the space of a week, our only hope is to take and hold as many of these nodes as we can and train there. We will not be able to master magic as quickly as Cadet Skywing did at the Prismatic City, but the rate of our learning should be greatly accelerated. If we're forced to fight, making a stand at these nodes will give us the best chance of victory."

Another general stood, indicating that he had a question. "Yes, General Nazoa?" the king asked.

General Nazoa nodded. "If the location of these magical nodes is such widespread knowledge, why haven't the other kingdoms around us simply taken them all over?"

"The locations are actually not widespread knowledge," Ennazar explained. "This map shows the ones we know about, but more are occasionally found, and their locations are usually closely kept secrets. If we were to find one in the Very Large Forest, for instance, we would take every precaution to make sure Exclaimovia didn't find out about it. So kingdoms like Claira and Esteria, which could have captured a number of nodes closer to Introvertia, have declined to do so, for two reasons. First, with us relatively weak due to refusing to use magic, they had no need to risk provoking us. It wasn't as if we were going to fight them for the node, but if we looked up one day and noticed that Claira held six to eight seemingly random locations in the hinterland between their kingdom and ours, we would probably ask why, and we may discover the nexus nodes on those locations, which Claira would not want." Ennazar folded his hands behind his back. "We do not need to be similarly concerned with secrecy at the moment, in my opinion. Yes, if we take these nodes to train on them, it's *possible* Claira may discover one they didn't know about. However, it's a *certainty* that Exclaimovia has threatened us with war. In my judgment the juice is worth the squeeze."

He paused, as if more nervous about this than about anything he had yet said. "I am sure there are other spellcasters in Introvertia who share my story, who have been training the magical arts in secret. If we can find them promptly, we should enlist their help. However, we must also consider the possibility that the two cadets in this room are two of the most powerful spellcasters currently in the kingdom. If there are unknown nexus lines or even nodes in Introvertia, which were known in ancient times but have been lost to history, Cadets Skywing and Ravenwood may be the only two with enough magical ability to help locate them. I would recommend that both cadets be assigned the mission of locating new nodes, and be given all possible support. It is now Thursday afternoon; I would suggest that by noon tomorrow, everyone who is to receive magical training should be sent to the nearest node, or possibly to a more distant node if its strength is enough to justify the added travel time. In the meantime, our conventional forces may deploy to their forward defensive positions and prepare for infantry and dragon warfare."

This plan was swiftly approved by the council, with no one opposing it. "Very well," King Jazan said decisively. "We speak with one voice. The mobilization order will go out at once. At noon tomorrow, the King's Army will deploy to their assigned nexus nodes. We will use the nodes within Introvertia wherever possible, and send only a few advance units to the more powerful nodes to the northeast. Cadet Skywing and Cadet Ravenwood will attempt to find new nodes within Introvertia." Eza could feel a buzz in the room. All the generals were eager to do their part to help the kingdom. "In that case," said the king, "you're all dismissed. Spend time with your families tonight."

Denavi Kiresti had expected glory and honor to feel a lot more...satisfying.

Saber Company had gotten a parade when they reentered the Clairan capital city of Arkiana. It was the same kind of parade Denavi had attended dozens of times growing up, maybe hundreds of times. Every time a unit returned from deployment, crowds lined the streets to cheer them on their way to Warrior Plaza, the square at the center of Arkiana where the Clairan Military Headquarters sat. Queen Revaki delivered an address about the nobility of self-sacrifice and the eternal memory of those who lived and died for Claira, and the crowd dispersed back to their homes, their lives unchanged except for those who'd lost loved ones.

It was probably supposed to feel meaningful for the soldiers, but Denavi just felt...*empty*.

She stood in Warrior Square, still in her filthy uniform, for a long time after the parade had ended, trying to figure out exactly what she was supposed to be feeling. Friends had been killed in front of her; others had been wounded, and Denavi could tell from their jumpiness and fear that it would be a long time before they were okay, if *okay* ever came back at all. Mothers were grieving sons today, wives grieving husbands, brothers grieving sisters. And for what? A parade?

Denavi's legs gave out and she sat down, her back against the statue of Ladri Arkian, the kingdom's founder. He was the original Noble Enlightened Warrior; the statue depicted him with a scroll in one hand and his magical sword Rainfire in the other. Arkian had been both a scholar and a fighter, known for quoting poetry as he led his troops, and that example had singlehandedly shaped Clairan society ever since. The kingdom had hardly stopped fighting wars against its neighbors for centuries – Esteria at first, until that kingdom had allied with Claira; then Norodrin to the northeast, Vagran to the north, and lately Telravia to the west. And after every battered company came back, they got the same parade, the same speech, and the families went through the same grief –

Denavi shook her head. Those feelings represented ingratitude of the highest order, and it was a good thing her thoughts weren't audible or else she would have been laughed out of the kingdom. She was a student in the Clairan Military Institute, a coveted spot that had been kept for her ever since her father had been killed. Oh, the dishonor that would be heaped on the Kiresti household if they knew she was letting this foolishness run through her head when she should be celebrating glorious victory over the Telravians...

But the memory came back, as strong and fierce as if it had happened the day before, when eight-year-old Denavi had flung the front door open with a giant smile on her face, expecting to see her father, only to be greeted by two stone-faced messengers from the Institute. Denavi had turned around, not understanding, just in time to see her mother fall to her knees, then shake her head several times before standing, fighting back tears, and thanking the messengers. That was it. Her father was gone. Life would never be the same.

Sometimes Denavi wished she could remember the last hug her father had ever given her. On days like this it made her sad that she couldn't. Was this really going to be her life? An endless series of deployments, hoping she was one of the lucky ones who returned to get a parade? Was this really what the life of an entire kingdom was supposed to be about?

A crowd was gathering on the opposite end of the square where the speaking podium was always set up. Denavi pushed to her feet and forced herself to walk that direction, aware that her uniform was filthy and stained and her hair was matted. People nodded to her as they passed, and one girl stared in open-mouthed awe. "Is that a real soldier, mommy?" the girl asked the woman next to her.

"It sure looks like it, sweetie. If you study hard in school, maybe you can be a soldier too one day."

Denavi smiled weakly.

But the man at the podium was addressing the crowd, which spared Denavi from having to respond. "Friends!" the man shouted authoritatively. "I come to you today with most dire news, news which spells disaster for Clairan society unless my words are heeded and acted upon!"

This got the crowd's attention, including Denavi's.

"My name is Azanna," the man said. "I am

Introvertian by birth, though I fled that kingdom long ago. I could not bear the deceitfulness of the Introvertian heart, the degree to which lying and hiding one's true motives are not merely encouraged but rewarded. My friends, I was grieved to my very core to find out that these same Introvertians have now reintroduced magic into their society! Just think, Clairans, consider what these Introvertians will do with their newfound power. Do you believe they will be content to live in their quiet corner of the world, minding their own business? No! They will seek out your destruction, Clairans, and the destruction of all who have ever raised a finger against their way of life!"

Azanna paused, pressing a hand to his chest as if reliving a painful memory. "I had the misfortune of meeting a particular Introvertian recently. No doubt you have heard the tale of the Introvertian and Exclaimovian who worked together to return hundreds of dragons to Introvertia. It was these two whom I met in the wilderness, as they were on the way to complete their theft. I did nothing more than ask if I could assist them when the Introvertian boy attacked me, and the Exclaimovian girl, doubtless under some kind of Introvertian mind control or witchcraft, used powerful elemental magic to incinerate my dragon!"

This drew gasps from the crowd, many of whom had

read tales of the ancient battles and knew how hardy dragons were supposed to be.

"Just think!" Azanna shouted, his finger in the air. "Just think what will happen if Introvertia conquers your kingdom! They will force you to live your lives in silence, as they do. Your children will never know the joy of laughing as they play in the streets! You will live in constant fear of judgment from those who never tell you their true thoughts. Claira has been fortunate, these many centuries, that Introvertia has been content to keep to themselves. But now that they have magic back, who will stand against their wrath? Only the brave armies of Claira, my friends! And stand you must!"

A cheer went up from the crowd. Those Introvertians sounded horrible, Denavi thought. Maybe *that* was why Claira needed to fight. The Telravians were awful people, a society obsessed with dark magic, and Introvertia didn't sound much better. If Claira didn't fight to keep those kinds of monsters from overrunning the world, who would?

A chill ran up her back. What would happen if those two kingdoms ever *allied* with each other?

Denavi stood a little straighter. She was a warrior of the kingdom of Claira, and she would wear the uniform proudly.

SIX

"Spend time with your families," King Jazan had said, and Eza obeyed the order. He and Cammie had left the castle and headed straight for Eza's house, where his father, Ezarra, was just getting home from work. The whole Skywing family had been dragon-companions for hundreds of years, and Ezarra's red dragon, Neemie, was waiting for all of them outside in the garden. Just a few weeks ago, Neemie had been three feet tall, able to comfortably stand on Eza's shoulders, and such a weak fire-breather that she would have had trouble lighting a candle. Now, after nearly a month of spending time with Eza and Cammie and being nourished by the magical energy they gave off, she had grown by nearly a foot and could spew flame almost like the dragons of old.

Aleiza must have heard Neemie's chatter, because she too came winging out of the backyard, swooping down next to Eza and nuzzling his hand as he squeezed the back of her neck. "Hey, girl," he told her. He hadn't figured out how much spoken language she understood, and he could communicate with her through the mind link (thoughts and impressions, at least, not specific words), but he often spoke to her out loud so Cammie didn't feel excluded. "And hi, dad!" He ran and jumped into his father's arms, although he was so tall now that his toes scraped the ground and he was pretty sure he heard his father's knees creaking. Someday soon he wouldn't be able to do that anymore, but today wasn't the day.

"Hi, Eza," Ezarra said warmly. "Hello, Cammie."

She accepted a hug from him as well. "Good afternoon, Mr. Skywing."

"This is a welcome surprise. Would you like to come help me make dinner? We can get some bread started, and I think I have some onala meat marinating."

Cammie was the first one to smile. "We'd love to."

The kitchen was a bustle of activity for the next hour as all three of them dodged around each other, reaching for ingredients and mixing things and building the wood fire. Cooking had gotten a lot easier now that they had dragons who could light the flame and stoke it whenever it got low, Eza had to admit. Some days when he was feeling exceptionally lazy, he'd just set the meat on a stone table and let the dragons fire-grill it right there on the spot. The dragons hadn't quite managed to bake a loaf of bread without turning it into a black brick, though.

Eza knew Cammie loved her family, and he knew it had hurt to leave them behind, even though she hadn't been given a choice in the matter. It always made him happy to spend time at home and let her be around him and his father. It wasn't the same as her real family – it never would be – but it might take a little bit of the pain away for a little while, and that was okay.

After dinner, with the sun going down and their bellies full of food, Eza and his father and Cammie sat on sofas in the living room, singing and telling stories. Cammie had told Eza once that Exclaimovians always ended their dinner with tales and songs, so that had become the family's new tradition. Cammie's stories were always hilarious; Exclaimovians prized storytelling almost as a form of currency, and Cammie was like a champion swordfighter, thrusting with descriptions and parrying with dialogue before slicing hard with a hilarious punchline or a breathtaking plot twist. She'd admitted to Eza back when they were on their first adventure that she'd never actually finished telling any of her stories before meeting him, because Exclaimovians were so fond of interrupting each other that someone would always butt in with a new story before she got to the good part of her own.

"Tell a story next, dad," Eza said excitedly.

Ezarra smiled. "What do you want to hear? Something from the Dragon Academy, or maybe from my Ranger days?"

"The Company Games are coming up next month at

the Academy. Did you ever compete in them?"

Ezarra tried to keep from laughing, but failed. "In a manner of speaking. I was instrumental in securing victory for Sun Company during my fifth year."

"What event did you win?"

"Ah..." Ezarra chuckled to himself. "The bathroom dash?"

"That's not a real event," protested Eza, looking at Cammie.

"No," Ezarra conceded. "However, you know how Victory Company students are. They're so smug about everything; they act like winning is their birthright."

"It is right there in the name," Cammie pointed out.

"True. But you can compete without being obnoxious about winning, right? Victory Company has never known how to do that. So it was the night before the final day of the games, and Kiezan Olaza, Victory's best sharpshooter, was expected to win the archery contest. He could have done it with one hand tied behind his back and pulling the arrow with his teeth; he really was that good. But he spent *all day* letting us all know how badly he was going to beat us and how Victory were going to celebrate after they won."

Eza looked over at Cammie. *Bathroom dash?* he mouthed.

Cammie shrugged.

"So," Ezarra said with a mischievous smile, "I was Sun Company, right. We love having fun; we love laughter. And we love a good prank. So I had been paying attention in survivalship class, and I knew of a particular plant that had...very strong laxative effects."

"No, you didn't," Eza said, laughing in anticipation.

"I did," Ezarra answered, obviously still proud. "I ran out after dinner, while there was still enough light. I had to go about a mile outside the city gates before I found some, and it was dark by the time I got back. I ground it down to a colorless powder, got the powder into a glass tube without accidentally touching myself in the process, and kept the tube on me until the next morning."

"How did you get it into his food without him noticing?" Cammie said excitedly.

"I'm getting there," Ezarra said. Cammie seemed to realize she'd just let her inner Exclaimovian slip out, and she covered her mouth. Eza could tell from the corners of her eyes that she was still smiling, though.

"I had to pass his table to get to mine anyway," Ezarra continued. "So I tripped, right, and I *accidentally* spilled the powder all over his breakfast. He didn't see it happen because he was turned the other way talking to some friends. I apologized for stumbling into his bench, and somehow managed to keep from laughing until I was back at my own table. But even then we couldn't laugh too hard, because someone would have known we were up to something. I swear to you, Eza, there were tears in my eyes as I watched him eat his breakfast. I felt like my entire body was going to explode from holding in all the laughter. He ate every last crumb off his plate and *licked it clean*." He saw Cammie's look of disbelief and held up his hand. "I promise I am not making any of this up."

"I believe you."

"I couldn't handle that, though. I ran back to the Sun barracks, which as you know are clear on the other side of Carnazon, and I laughed for a solid fifteen minutes. There were tears and snot and I was gasping for air. It was ugly." Ezarra considered his next words. "Not nearly as ugly as what happened in the Victory Company lavatory over the course of the next two hours, I'm told."

Eza was done; he laughed so hard he rolled off the couch. "I never knew you had it in you, dad," he said when he was finally able to breathe again.

"Without Kiezan, Victory didn't stand a chance. One of our girls won the competition and Sun won the Company Games. As far as I'm aware, only four or five Sun Company cadets ever knew that story, and now you do too."

Cammie nudged Eza in the ribs. "We'll have to keep

that in mind, won't we?"

"What plant was it?" Eza asked, and then smiled when his father hesitated. "It was connara root, wasn't it? It was. I can see you trying not to laugh."

"It was," Ezarra confessed.

Telling a worthy follow-up to that story would have been extremely difficult, so neither Cammie nor Eza tried. After a few moments of silence, Ezarra cleared his throat. "I heard about the mobilization order."

"They're not sending us to the front lines," Eza said immediately. "Our mission is to scout magical nexus nodes here in Introvertia."

Ezarra nodded; he probably didn't know what nexus nodes were, Eza realized. "That sounds important. I'm glad they chose you two."

"Do you really think there's going to be a war?" Cammie asked quietly.

"I don't know," admitted Ezarra. "I hope not. Introvertia has always done everything we can to live at peace with other nations. As far as I know we've never started a war, ever, in our entire history. All we want is to be left alone. My hope is that Exclaimovia – and their allies, if all that talk was true and not just bluster – will see how strong we are and think twice."

Cammie snorted a laugh. "You'll be lucky if you can get my people to think once, never mind twice."

Eza smiled at the joke, but he could hear the pain in her voice. "What if you wrote to your family?"

"I've wanted to, but I don't know how to get a message through. It's not like people regularly travel from Introvertia to Exclaimovia."

"My uncle Tully does. He's a trader. He meets about once a week with an Exclaimovian named –"

"Kalek," Cammie said suddenly. "I know Kalek. I always made him tell me stories about the Silent Ones." She glanced at Eza, a little embarrassed. "That was my nickname for your people."

"Really?" Eza asked, trying to stifle a giggle.

"Hey, you called us the Kingdom of People Yelling and Having No Concept of Personal Space."

"Still do sometimes."

"HEY!"

Eza slid over quickly, sitting on the arm of the couch in case her fingers decided to get all pokey.

"It's kind of true, though," she conceded.

"Kind of *really* true."

"That's a good idea, though. I'll write them a letter tonight, and we can take it to your uncle tomorrow morning on our way back to Carnazon. He lives here in Tranquility, right?"

"Yeah, but on the other side. We'll have to leave early."

Ezarra stood and stretched. "I'm going to bed. In case you're gone before I wake up, be safe. I love you both."

Eza went in for a hug, and Cammie joined him. "I love you, dad," Eza said.

Cammie seemed like she wanted to say something, but she just swallowed.

Ezarra went upstairs, leaving Eza and Cammie to themselves downstairs. "Want to read together?" Eza asked.

"No, thank you. I think I want to be alone." She saw Eza's eyes nearly pop out, and corrected herself quickly. "Not quiet-alone. Singing to myself alone and talking to myself alone."

"Are you okay?"

"Of *course* I'm not okay," she snapped. It was the first flash of attitude Eza had seen out of her in almost a week, and it shocked him after how well she'd handled Razan and Anneka the afternoon before. He blinked, hurt, but he knew even as he did that she wasn't mad at *him*. She was mad at other things and he just happened to be there for her to yell at.

But if that's what made her feel better, then he could handle it.

"My family is *fifty miles away* and I miss them so much and now there might be a war, and I'm expected to help you beat my people, except they're *not even my people anymore* because they decided they don't want me around, and now I have my best friend asking me *whether I'm okay...*"

Eza didn't know how to react. He wanted to smile reassuringly, but she might think he was making fun of her. So he watched and said nothing.

"Don't get me wrong. I'm glad I did what I did. Those dragons were suffering and we did the right thing by releasing them. I just wish we could have done the right thing without people getting mad about it." She put her hands on her hips and looked at the ceiling. "But I guess that happens a lot, doesn't it? You can never please everybody. You just have to do what you know is right, and the right people will agree with you. Which is why I'm here. One group of people kicked me out for doing the right thing, and another took me in for doing the right thing. I guess I know where I'd rather be." She glanced at Eza. "Great talk."

"I said nothing," Eza said, his palms spread in protest.

"Yeah. Great talk. You Silent Ones are really useful sometimes."

Cammie smiled at him and winked as she headed up the stairs to her bedroom. Astounding, Eza thought. She really did seem to feel better after spewing all her feelings on him. Some days he thought he almost had

Cammie figured out, and then she went and did something like this.

He followed her upstairs and got himself ready for bed. Cammie was humming in the adjacent bedroom, and for a while Eza was worried he wouldn't be able to get to sleep, since he slept so lightly. But the sound was relaxing to him, and in minutes he was gone.

It was nearly noon before Cammie and Eza, with Aleiza in tow, hustled up to Mazaren Fortress on the northwest side of Tranquility. Eza had spent the whole trip giving Cammie history and geography lessons. Named for the ancient hero of Introvertia, the citadel had been built at the same time as Carnazon, but had seen much less combat due to being on the opposite side of the city from where an invading army would arrive. Tranquility was massive by Introvertian standards, nearly fifteen miles across and ten miles from the Rapidly Flowing River in the south to the twin fortresses in the north. Introvertia as a whole formed a rounded square, about sixty miles east to west and sixty miles north to south. Most of the population lived within a narrow strip along the Rapidly Flowing River, which began in the Cloudscraper Mountains in the north and wrapped around the west side of the kingdom before running the entire length of the south and then on to

Exclaimovia. Farmsteads and logging villages and mining towns were scattered throughout the kingdom, but there was also a lot of wilderness between the river and the northern cities of Courage, nestled in the Cloudscrapers, and Resolve, at the foot of the Cloudscrapers on Introvertia's northeastern border near Telravia.

"They're going to deport you to Exclaimovia if you keep talking," Cammie teased.

"This isn't small talk. This is important."

"I know. You're just fun to tease."

A full company of Introvertian scouts had been assigned to them: thirty cavalry, fifty infantry, and twenty archers. Enough horses waited nearby to carry all of them plus Cammie and Eza. To Cammie's surprise, Colonel Ennazar was also waiting for them. Eza saluted immediately, and Cammie followed a moment later.

"At ease, Cadets," the colonel said. "Let's talk nexus nodes for a moment. In an ideal world I would have several months to train you on how to find them and how to recognize when you're near one, but we don't have months. We have..." He squinted at the sun. "About five minutes. So here goes. You probably noticed, Ezalen, that when you were at the Prismatic City, the magic seemed to flow easily out of you. When you tried the same magic again elsewhere, things were more difficult, almost as if you were...trying to suck the power through a thin straw. Does that sound right?"

"Yes, sir," Eza said, looking surprised. "It felt exactly like that."

"As you heard me say yesterday, the Prismatic City is a special case. Five different nexus lines intersect there; you won't feel the effect as strongly anywhere else in the five kingdoms that we know about. But even on a node where two or three lines meet, you'll notice a certain...tingling, I suppose. Magic will be easier to use, and the spells will be more powerful with less effort."

"So we just wander around casting spells until we find a place where it's easy?" Cammie clarified.

Colonel Ennazar smiled. "Not quite. First, I want you to investigate one of the nodes that I happened to come across on my travels. I believe it's at the intersection of two lines. Then go to the two other locations I've marked on this map and see how they feel compared with the first one. It might turn out all three are two-line nodes, but I have reason to suspect that one of them is a three-line node. That would help our training immensely." He looked to Eza, and then to Cammie. "In an ideal world, I would have been doing this myself over the past five years. I believe that a mage as strong as I am could have found the nodes by feel, without having to break the old laws by casting spells. Perhaps I could've had all the nodes in Introvertia mapped by now. But I never imagined that our fate as a kingdom would be riding on something like this."

Cammie didn't know what to say, so Eza chipped in another "Yes, sir."

"When you get there," Colonel Ennazar added, "feel free to train everyone who's with you in whichever kind of magic they want to learn. I honestly don't know how useful magic will be to the soldiers, since they've already trained their formations and battle plans, and having them start using magic might hurt more than help. But I think we'll all have to learn a little magic eventually, and if we can get our army even a little bit more powerful before the war..." He smiled grimly. "Everything will help."

"We'll do all we can," promised Cammie.

"I expect no less of Dragon Academy cadets. If you keep your schedule, you'll even be back before the Spring Equinox Festival. You're in good hands; Captain Mozara is more than capable. Dismissed!"

The horses led them swiftly northwest, toward the interior of the kingdom. Eza had said that there were two main roads that went north, one from Tranquility to Resolve, and the other parallel to it but about thirty miles away, heading toward Courage. For most of their length, the roads ran through very thick forest, and the only settlements were at about fifteen-mile intervals, representing an easy day's travel for someone on foot. Farms and logging camps sprawled out from the settlements, but there were still large stretches of the interior where no one regularly went.

It looked like that's where Colonel Ennazar's map was taking them.

The horses covered ground much faster than the company could have on foot, even through the forests, which were made up of tall mature trees and were largely free from underbrush. By dinnertime they had traveled a significant distance. The forest mostly looked the same, except for a few small streams the horses had forded. Cammie might have wondered whether they were just going in circles except that she trusted Eza's Ranger skills – and the other hundred soldiers they were with, of course.

"Why are we stopping for dinner?" Cammie asked as the sun began to slink toward the horizon. "I thought we were in a hurry."

"It's for the horses," Eza told her. "We're not the ones who need a break, but they've been picking their way over rough terrain all day. It's kind of amazing we've come as far as we have. I think the node is only fifteen more miles that way."

"I don't suppose these folks would be up for songs

after dinner?" Cammie said hopefully.

Eza smiled at the thought. "Probably not, although I bet they'd be okay with stories. I bet none of them have ever met an Exclaimovian before."

Eza was right. Cammie told the story of how she and Eza had gotten the dragons back, but even as the story stretched on for one hour and then two and the last of the sunlight disappeared, the soldiers still listened intently, watching Cammie's face and gestures in the flicker of the cooking fire that was still burning. When she reached the climactic moment, where Eza and Cammie had marched back through the gates of Tranquility with a formation of seven hundred dragons overhead, a cheer went up – not much of a cheer by Exclaimovian standards, of course, but a murmur of approval and a smattering of applause. Cammie stood to bow. "Thank you, thank you."

"Miss Cammaina Ravenwood," Eza said, as if presenting her to a packed theater house. The applause got louder and several of the soldiers gave her a standing ovation.

Cammie elbowed Eza. "Stop it. I'm blushing."

"Then blush."

Cammie had to admit she enjoyed performing again, and that thought put an idea in her head. Maybe she could find a theater company to join in Tranquility.

Queen Annaya had been an actress, after all. Perhaps, if Cammie asked nicely, the queen might put in a kind word for her. *That* would give her the chance to really be herself, in a place where she would be not merely tolerated, but appreciated. She was happy at the Academy for now and didn't want to leave...maybe one day, though...

An even better thought came to her: what if she started a theater company *at the Academy itself*? She knew she could probably rope Eza into joining. Shanna was definitely loud enough for the stage. With a few other people, they could put on some of the Exclaimovian plays she'd performed – or even *write her own*. Excitedly she rolled over to tell Eza all about her plans, and he listened with wide eyes and a big smile as the soldiers around them set up their sleeping bags in a defensive perimeter. Eza and Cammie were left alone in the middle, and a long time later, when Cammie had finished telling Eza her dreams for the future, she put her head on the ground and let the real dreams take over.

SEVEN

Eza awoke in the gray pre-dawn, heart slamming in his chest and panic gripping him. This happened to him a couple of times a week, sometimes after a nightmare and sometimes for no reason that he could figure out. No one else was awake at the moment, so he sat up, slithering out of his sleeping bag. It was chilly without the sun to warm the ground, and Cammie was halfway out of her bag as usual, her arms spread crazily on the ground. Eza draped his sleeping bag over her upper body, teeth chattering a bit as he reached into his pack for another layer of clothing.

Also in the pack was the map that Colonel Ennazar had given him. Eza laid it on the ground, tracing it with his finger so that it appeared larger in the air like the map he had drawn in the throne room two days before. If there were any patterns on it, any hidden shapes, maybe he would be able to see them. Maybe he could find another three-line node, or perhaps even a four-line. That would change the shape of the entire war.

If there was a war. Eza knew that the Exclaimovians were fond of bluster. He'd seen Cammie do it more times than he could remember, changing the topic or suddenly saying something ridiculous when it seemed she wasn't getting her way. Threatening a three-front invasion was exactly the sort of over-the-top thing the Exclaimovians could always be counted on to do.

But even if Exclaimovia never invaded, this whole matter of the magical nodes would change the course of life in Introvertia. Anyone who wanted to could come to a node and train their own magical abilities. It was a gift, Eza thought, a pure gift.

He rocked back on his heels, his heart still beating unpleasantly fast, and he closed his eyes, reaching out into the gray gloom with his other four senses. There was the chill on his skin, and in his nose and lungs as he breathed in. The taste of the forest was on his tongue, the dirt and whatever else was carried on the breeze. The faint whooshing of a breeze brought the smell of evergreen needles to his nose. Opening his eyes again, he picked out the sleeping bodies of the soldiers around him, and Cammie next to him. Slowly he began to calm down. The panic feeling was dissipating.

In an hour or so the whole camp was moving, even Cammie, who rolled up Eza's sleeping bag and handed it back to him. "Sleep well?" he asked her.

Cammie just growled at him, which made Eza double over in laughter.

"I'm glad one of us thinks it's funny," she said.

"It's not funny," Eza corrected. "It's hilarious."

After a huge breakfast (during which, Eza noticed with approval, Cammie used the spices he'd given her) the company set out again, following Captain Mozara. They were only a few hours' trot from where the node was supposed to be, but the closer they got, the denser the forest became. Aleiza was hardly able to fly through the thick trees, and had taken a seat behind Eza on his horse. It was a good thing she was light. Colonel Ennazar's map showed a ribbon of hills in this area; it seemed to Eza that most of the nodes were in hilly or mountains areas, but he didn't know enough about magic to understand why. The horses took them up one hill, then down the opposite side into a valley so deep that only a few patches of blue sky were visible through the trees. A stream ran across the bottom of the valley, which the horses forded easily, then began the difficult trek up the opposite hill.

"Do you feel that?" Cammie asked quietly.

Eza did. There was a sort of crackling in the air, a strange energy – sort of like what he'd felt at the Prismatic City, but on that occasion he'd been so excited about meeting an Artomancer that he hadn't paid much attention. "It's getting stronger as we go this way," he observed. Aleiza was radiating contentment; whatever that energy was, she liked it, or maybe it just reminded her of her old home.

A deep ravine yawned open in front of them, winding down and around, going deeper and deeper as it became thinner. After a quarter mile, it was so narrow that only four horses could go side by side, and the company was stuck following Cammie and Eza at the front of the line. The crackling was stronger now. Eza felt like any spell he cast would be twice as strong and twice as effortless as usual.

There – something like a cave appeared on the left side of the ravine. It wasn't a natural cave, though; maybe it had been once, but the entrance was squared off, with intricate decorations carved around it. Someone had marked this place deliberately, Eza thought. This had to be it. They'd found a nexus node.

At that moment the horses screamed under them and wheeled crazily. Aleiza instantly sprang into the air, and Eza yanked his feet from the stirrups and leaped to the ground, grabbing the reins of Cammie's horse and trying to calm it. He couldn't; the horse was thoroughly panicked by – by *something*. "Jump!" Eza told Cammie, and she stared at him with wide eyes for half a moment before hurling herself free of the horse. Her dismount wasn't as graceful as Eza's; she crashed into him and he leaned against her, protectively wrapping her in both arms to keep her from falling over. "Are you okay?" he asked.

Cammie nodded wordlessly.

But the rest of the company was struggling with their own horses, and in moments there was a stampede, the soldiers pushing themselves to the walls of the narrow ravine as the horses whinnied and kicked each other and stamped their feet. Some at the rear took off back the way the company had come, while Cammie's and Eza's and some others from the front ran past the mouth of the cave –

A deafening roar shattered the air, echoing a million times off the narrow walls of the ravine, and a dozen bears burst from the cave, smashing into the horses and mauling them to pieces. The horses' screams joined the roaring, and horse parts sailed through the air as the bears tore them limb from limb.

"Bears" wasn't the right word, Eza suddenly realized. The things *looked* like bears, but they were as tall on all fours as the horses were. Aleiza, who had been weaving back and forth overhead, screamed down toward them and strafed them with a powerful gush of flame, searing the hair off several of them and sending one to the ground smoking. But then one of the bears stood up on its rear legs – it had to be at least eleven feet tall, Eza noticed in shock – and a tangle of blue-white energy erupted from its paws, straight at Aleiza. She was arching upward at the end of her strafing run and didn't see it coming. Panicking, Eza reached out through his mind link and told her, *"LEFT!"* Without hesitation she swooped to the left, as far as the tight confines of the ravine would allow, and the energy ball sizzled past her into the sky.

"Did that bear just cast a spell?" Cammie screamed.

"Take it down!" Captain Mozara ordered, and arrows from the archers twanged past Eza and Cammie. The bears hardly seemed to notice. Cammie let fly with an arc of lightning more powerful than Eza had ever seen her unleash – she must be terrified, he thought. The lightning pierced one bear, passed clean through it, and fried the one behind it too. Two down, Eza thought, ten to go.

When Eza was first learning Artomancy, his instructor, Gar, had told him that Artomancy was not an attack-minded school of magic. He would have to be more creative – but he also hadn't eaten since breakfast, so he didn't know how much energy he'd have inside him. If he didn't pace himself, he would end up exhausted and unable to fight.

Cammie didn't seem concerned about that; she screamed again, this time in anger rather than terror, and a fireball blasted out from her hands, reducing one bear to a seven-foot mound of ash on the spot. "Take it easy!" Eza shouted to her. "Don't –"

But Cammie was in her own world; she went up on

her toes like a dancer and actually twirled around as she shrieked and fired off another searing bolt of lightning. Eza stepped forward himself, aiming a bolt of blinding light directly at the eyes of the closest bear, which blinked and roared. At that instant, though, the remaining eight bears charged directly at him and Cammie.

Soldiers tried to shoulder their way in front of the two, but Eza held out his arms and blocked them. This was the hardest spell he knew how to cast, and if he did it wrong, or if he missed –

A shimmering door of multicolored light appeared in front of the bears. The first one ran headlong into it, dropping out from an exit door that was thirty feet above the ground, thudding hard onto the ravine floor. Then the rainbow door moved and swallowed the second bear, and the third, and the fourth. All of them plummeted from the exit door, landing almost on top of the first bear, and the others hurtled through as well, unable to stop themselves in time...

Cammie screeched and let fly another fireball moments later, which crashed into the mass of stunned bears. One burst apart into a hundred pieces as the ball of flame ignited inside it, and another's head melted when a lightning arc passed between its eyes. Then Aleiza was sailing down out of the sky again, wings tucked against her body, belching fire –

The huge bear stood up once more and fired off an energy ball even larger than its first one...but not at Aleiza. It was aimed at the soldiers behind Cammie and Eza, or maybe it had been aimed at Cammie and simply missed. The ground exploded and twenty soldiers flew into the air, bouncing off the walls of the ravine and landing on each other or hard on the ground.

That was the last straw for Cammie, who ran forward as if she were going to strangle the bears with her own hands. The giant bear reared up on its hind legs – did it have to recharge before casting another spell, or was it just confused? – and she had gotten to within six feet of it when she seemed to reach inside herself, and *a massive round shield made of lightning* appeared in front of her, then hurled itself out to smash into the remaining animals. The huge bear blew violently apart, splattering the walls of the ravine as well as Cammie and Eza and even Aleiza, who had chosen that moment to start another strafing run. Electricity crackled through the bear pieces as they lay on the ground.

Cammie sagged against Eza, her eyes drooping closed.

Between Cammie's attacks and Aleiza's assaults, only three bears remained, and they took off fleeing in the opposite direction, leaving behind silence and the groans of the wounded Introvertian soldiers. Eza moved in front of Cammie so that she was draped over him, and he held her wrists together in front of his neck. He'd seen her overextend herself before when using magic, and knew that she was in for a lengthy period of recovery. "We need to get to the cave," he shouted to the soldiers.

"What if there are more bears in there?" one of them asked.

"Then we'll have to fight them. Our orders are to take the node."

Thankfully, it didn't seem as if there were any other magical abominations in the cave, at least not in the first chamber that Eza entered. Magical lights on the walls flickered; they must have been lit for centuries, Eza realized with wonder, powered by the latent magical energy that coursed through the nexus lines and through the node itself. Apparently the energy was so strong that it had made those bears grow huge (just like it did to dragons, Eza thought) and had even given at least one of them the ability to cast spells. It was a shame they hadn't been able to tame those bears somehow. A spellcasting bear would be awfully useful on the battlefield.

He dragged Cammie to one corner of the chamber and leaned her against a wall while he unrolled his sleeping bags, laying one out and then easing her onto it before covering her with the other. She needed rest, he knew, but she also needed food. He was ravenously hungry himself just from the small amount of magic he'd used; he couldn't imagine how Cammie's body would be feeling when she woke up. Aleiza settled down next to Cammie, spreading her wings protectively over Cammie's head and feet. That brought a smile to Eza's face; Aleiza really didn't like Cammie and the sudden outbursts of noise that often came along with the Exclaimovian's presence, but the dragon seemed to understand that Cammie was special to Eza, so Aleiza treated her accordingly.

The rest of the company quickly secured the tunnel that led deeper into the cave, sliding a slab of stone across the gap and securing it with wooden beams that had been lying nearby. If there were animals or magical horrors deeper in the cave, they wouldn't easily be able to enter the chamber. More than twenty Introvertian soldiers had been injured by the bear's magical attacks, five of them seriously, but it seemed as if none of them were going to die. That was incredible, Eza thought. It was a shame there wasn't some kind of healing school of magic that could get them back on their feet sooner.

Apart from the beams they'd used to block the door, that front chamber was mostly empty. There was a fountain in the middle that was probably supposed to have water in it but didn't. It would have been smart to build a barricade across the front of the cave in case the bears came back, but Eza didn't see anything they could use for that. The soldiers would just have to guard it with their bodies.

He was about to open his mouth and ask the soldiers to retrieve some roasted bear meat from outside, but he suddenly second-guessed himself. Had the magic inside the bears changed their bodies somehow? Would it be harmful to eat their meat? Eza didn't know, and now probably wasn't the best time to try an experiment.

Cammie stirred, grimacing in pain, and Eza knelt next to her. "Drink something," he said, putting his canteen of water up to her mouth. She struggled to sit up, and he put his hand on the back of her neck, easing her forward.

"I feel...awful," she said, taking the canteen from him and holding it with shaking hands.

Her hair was thoroughly wild and some of it was hanging down into the corner of her mouth, so Eza put his hand on her temple, brushing the hair back. "Can you eat?"

Cammie took a long drink of water and gave a strangled moan. "You know how it feels. I'm starving but I feel like throwing up."

"Maybe some bread?" he offered. His backpack was just out of reach, so he used his leg and pulled it toward him with his toes. "Here."

With some difficulty, Cammie managed to get it down, and almost immediately she looked better. "I'm going to need all your food," she warned him. "Right now."

She spent the next hour eating everything that Eza could get her, from her own backpack and then from the supplies that the company had brought with them. True to her word, several times she looked like she was going to be sick, but she kept all the food down. Standing up was a different story. When she tried to push herself to her feet, her legs simply gave out under her; she fell onto Eza again and he eased her back to the floor.

"It's going to take a while to get your strength back," he said. "But...wow, Cammie. Your magic was *so strong*."

"Some of that was the node, I think. It really did feel effortless, just like Colonel Ennazar said it would." She hesitated. "But I was really, really scared, too. You know my magic kind of does its own thing when I'm feeling strong emotions. This was...the most scared I remember being since I roasted Azanna's dragon." Cammie looked up at Eza, worry on her face. "I really thought we might die. That's why the magic blew out of me like that."

Eza didn't know what to say, so he took her hand and squeezed it.

"When you feel better," he said at last, "I bet there are about a hundred people here who'd rather learn elemental magic than Artomancy. Fancy being a teacher?"

A weary smile leaped to her face. "Sounds great."

EIGHT

It took two precious days before the injured Introvertian soldiers were capable of moving. If the horses hadn't fled or been mauled by bears, moving the wounded would have been a lot easier, but since every soldier had to walk under his or her own power, rushing the recovery wasn't possible.

Cammie had occupied the time by teaching elemental magic to anyone who would listen – which, it turned out, was everyone. Being on a nexus node truly did make things a lot easier. At Carnazon, the students had been happy if they could make a flicker of sparks after their first lesson; here in the cave, several of the soldiers had been starting campfires after an hour of training.

But their orders from Colonel Ennazar had been to scout two different nodes and then report back, and they were already behind schedule. Four days had passed since they'd left Tranquility; they only had three left to find the second node, try to figure out if it might be a three-line node like Colonel Ennazar thought it might, and then get back. Privately, Cammie didn't see how it was possible.

She was packing to leave when she noticed Eza and Captain Mozara having a quiet conversation off to the side. Curiosity drew her over, and she stood next to Eza, half-expecting that he would tell her to quit being nosy. However, all he did was acknowledge her presence with a nod.

"If we send our wounded straight back to Tranquility, the rest of us will be able to move much more quickly," Captain Mozara said. "Time is of the essence. We have to get this figured out before Exclaimovia and their allies arrive in Introvertia."

"*If* they arrive," Eza corrected. "Besides, what if there are more magical creatures waiting for us at the next node? Colonel Ennazar thinks that node may be even stronger than the one we're currently on. What if we're attacked by something more powerful than those bears?"

"Do you think twenty wounded soldiers will make the difference in a fight like that?"

"Okay, but what if they're attacked by something else on the way back? If those bears come back, or some other animals ambush them? Our people wouldn't stand a chance; they wouldn't even be able to retreat."

"If they die and the rest of us find a three-line node that helps us win a war, I believe every single one of them would say that's an acceptable sacrifice."

Eza sighed. He didn't seem to like the idea of putting someone else's life in danger – even though he'd swordfought Azanna, snuck into Exclaimovia, infiltrated an underground burial crypt to steal back Introvertia's dragons, and put his body in front of Cammie's when those bears were coming at them. Personally, Cammie thought the captain's reasoning was sound, but it wasn't her business. At last Eza nodded. "Very well. Let's send the wounded back. They can take our report to the colonel." Captain Mozara moved away immediately, and Eza looked at Cammie, stress still on his face. "That's not fun."

"You made a good choice," she assured him.

That made a smile reach all the way to his green eyes. "Thanks."

Less than an hour later, part of the company was marching back toward Tranquility while the other part was continuing onward toward the next location Colonel Ennazar had marked on the map. It was about fifteen miles north of the first, a rough trek over the same broken and hilly terrain. Almost the entire day had passed before they threaded their way between two hills and the landscape opened in front of them, revealing a round lake about a half mile from one end to the other. In the middle sat an island, with something like a library built on top of it.

Cammie and Eza looked at each other. "The node is on that island?" she asked, pointing.

"It sure looks that way." Eza took a deep breath. "Do

you feel the energy, though? Look how far we are from the island, and how much stronger it is than the last one."

"How are we supposed to get there? Do you think we can use your rainbow door?"

"That's a great idea," Eza said. "I've never used it over such a long distance, though. I went sixty feet when we were rescuing the dragons, and I think that's about as far as I can do it. Of course I could go further here because of the nexus node, but I don't know how much further. I'd have to try it out on land before trying to move us out that far over water."

The company halted near the shore of the lake and formed a semicircular defensive perimeter while Eza set about pushing his Artomancy magic to its limits. Being close to such a strong node made things easier for him, no doubt, and after fifteen minutes he had managed to send himself and Cammie almost, but not quite, far enough to get to the center of the lake.

"I keep coming up about thirty feet short," Eza said in frustration. "And I don't want to cast the spell too many more times because I might run out of energy. I need to eat something now, anyway." He sat down heavily by the side of the lake, munching on some dried meat. "What if," he said suddenly through a mouthful, "you used your elemental magic to raise the ground and make a stepping stone for us?"

Cammie stared at him, mouth open. "A land bridge, you mean?"

"Why not? It should work, right?"

"I mean...I've never done it before, but I guess it should." She looked skeptically at the water. "How deep do you think it is there? Like...how much effort is this actually going to take?"

Eza tossed her the rest of his meat stick. "Better chow down."

Most of the soldiers were playing with their own magic by this point, starting fires for others to put out with water spells. "What if we had some of them help us?" Cammie asked.

Understanding dawned on Eza's face. "Amazing idea." He got the soldiers' attention. "I want one of you to try using earth magic to raise the ground here at the edge of the lake, just enough to make a little step out into the water. Then someone else try the next step, and the next. When the water gets too deep for one person to do it alone, they'll raise the ground as much as they can and the next person will pick up where they left off. Okay?"

Eza had never seen trained combat soldiers look so positively giddy. Before long, a walkway about forty feet long had formed, leading out toward the lake. "That's far enough," Eza told the troops. Cammie saw shoulders slump in disappointment, so Eza added quickly, "You don't want to push yourselves too much. You all saw what happened to Cammie back at the nexus node. If that happens to all of us, we're in trouble."

Cammie followed Eza out onto the walkway, which was still wet; mud squelched underneath her boots and in some places she sank down up to her ankles. They reached the very end of the land bridge and Eza eyeballed the island in the middle of the lake, closer now but still a huge distance away. "Can you do it?" Cammie asked quietly.

Eza's only answer was to take a deep breath, close his eyes, and draw with his hands.

A bright shimmering circle appeared in front of him. Cammie leaned around it to try and find the other side...

There it was, on the island, about five feet from the water. "I'll go first," Eza said, and he stepped through the rainbow door. Immediately he popped out on the other side, standing on the island and beckoning Cammie through. She took one big step in –

And was immediately on the other side, faster even than blinking. Eza collapsed the rainbow doors and she craned her neck to see the Introvertian soldiers by the lake and Aleiza flying toward the island. Cammie waved at them to let them know she and Eza had arrived safely, then turned back toward the center of the island.

There was an almost tangible crackling in the air now. The Prismatic City had felt this way, even *more* so, but at the time she'd been thinking about other things – like getting away from Azanna and his band of riders that were trying to kill her. By the time she and Eza had met Gar the Artomancer, she couldn't remember feeling the crackle anymore; had she gotten used to it? Was the same thing going to happen here?

There was an awful lot about magic that she didn't know, and maybe an awful lot about magic that *nobody* knew.

Eza was already heading for the building that looked like a library, so she hustled to catch up to him. Just as he approached the outer wall, something burst up through the top of it. It was *huge,* whatever it was, maybe twice the size of Aleiza, eighteen feet tall and with a twenty-foot wingspan. Cammie's eyes focused better and she gasped. It was unmistakably a dragon.

Immediately Cammie began drawing on her magic, ready to cast a spell at a moment's notice, but Eza put a warning hand on her shoulder. "Don't," he said.

The dragon soared into the sky, silver scales glinting. It saw Aleiza and roared; Aleiza roared right back. The two dragons stared each other down, and then the huge one took off, soaring into the evening sky and catching the sun's rays, making its silver scales reflect the orange and purple of the sky. Cammie could hardly breathe. "What was that?" she asked.

"A dragon," Eza said. "A really big dragon."

"But...how? Colonel Ennazar said this was a three-line node. Aleiza grew up on a three-line node and she's not that large. That thing was *HUGE*."

"I don't know. Maybe Aleiza grew up near the node but not right on it. Maybe there's some other magic going on that we don't know about." Eza held out his empty hands. "Once upon a time somebody probably knew the answers to all these questions, but we haven't had magic for eight centuries."

"Fair point."

"Either way it looks like we got what we came for. This is definitely a stronger node than the first one, just like Colonel Ennazar thought. I would never have been able to send a rainbow door that far on my own."

"Does that mean we go back to give our report, then?"

"I think we should. If Exclaimovia is going to invade, we want to be in Tranquility when it happens."

Cammie's chest tightened. "You've been saying all along you don't think Exclaimovia is going to start a war."

"I don't think they will," Eza said quickly. "I'm sorry. I didn't mean to upset you. I just –"

"*You* didn't upset me. My people upset me when they decided they'd rather invade Introvertia than let me live a happy life."

Sometimes she could just *tell* when Eza didn't know what to say. It was like his confusion was audible. "I appreciate you being quiet at times like this," she blurted. "In Exclaimovia they'd all be saying stupid stuff like *don't worry,* as if that ever helped anyone, or *it's going to be okay* when they have no clue whether it will or not. You're too honest for all of that. Sometimes it drives me nuts when you're quiet, but sometimes it's the right response."

"Good," Eza said with a laugh. "Because if you'd forced me to say something, it probably would have been a nursery rhyme. Ready to head back?"

"Let's do it."

Eza drew his rainbow door again, and Cammie stepped through, just barely making it onto the extended walkway the soldiers had made. As Eza was about to come through, though, an incredible roar shook the entire lake, and Cammie whirled around to see the silver dragon return. The rainbow door faltered and vanished. Panicked, Cammie looked for Eza on the far shore. Aleiza was circling over his head, and the silver dragon was getting closer, closer –

Eza drew the door one final time, but the other end

wasn't far enough. If he walked through it now, he would fall about five feet short of the walkway, and Cammie had no clue how deep the water was here. But Eza got a running start and leaped through anyway, splashing into the water a short distance from Cammie.

She dropped to her stomach, mud instantly soaking into her clothes, and she reached a hand toward Eza. He was flailing toward the walkway, wet clothes and all, and he reached for Cammie with one hand while grabbing the walkway with his other hand. In two seconds he was standing up straight, drenched and muddy, while the silver dragon soared gracefully over the island. Aleiza was hurrying toward them, and Eza looked at Cammie. "The dragon doesn't care about us. It was just startled. It didn't like us being in its home."

"I'm not sure I blame it."

Despite Eza's assurances, Cammie watched the dragon over her shoulder as she made her way back to the shore where the soldiers were waiting. "We found what we came for," Eza told them. "Let's get back to Tranquility as quickly as we can."

That was easier said than done, with no horses and over broken terrain. Eza and Captain Mozara quickly decided that the best thing would not be to head directly southeast toward Tranquility, but rather to go straight east out of the hills and forest and join up with the main road, wherever it happened to be. They kept traveling after sunset, which was no easy task considering the thickness of the forest and the rockiness of the ground, and emerged from the trees onto a plain about three hours before midnight. The boulevard that led from Tranquility to Resolve was visible in the distance, but that was tomorrow's problem; the company made camp for the night.

Even aided by the wide, flat, paved trade road, it still took them half a day to reach Tranquility; they would arrive on the sixth day after being sent out, almost exactly as Colonel Ennazar had ordered them. On the morning of that final day, Eza had strapped his report to Aleiza's leg and sent the dragon ahead of them to the city. When they arrived, Colonel Ennazar was waiting for them, a huge smile on his face.

"I'm impressed!" he greeted them, shaking Eza's hand and then Cammie's. "And, of course, I'm surpassingly pleased that my suspicions were confirmed. We have a three-line node right here in Introvertia! I'll be taking a company of soldiers there at once to begin training. We will, of course, watch out for the dragon you spoke of. If it could be enlisted to our purposes, that would be even better, but if not, we will accommodate."

He was blathering like an Exclaimovian, Cammie thought mildly, but of course he was probably just excited. She would have been too, in his shoes, if she'd been forced to hide her magical ability for – how old was he, anyway, about thirty-five? – yes, for decades, and was only now respected and admired for it. He'd earned the right to strut a little bit, in her opinion.

"What are our next orders, sir?" Eza asked, snapping to a salute.

"You'll both be pleased to know that there is no sign of an Exclaimovian attack – nor of anything unusual from Claira or Esteria. We have our entire Ranger corps deployed in the Very Large Forest, in the Impassable Mountains, and to the northeast between us and Claira. So far they have reported absolutely nothing. Exclaimovia's threatened war has not materialized, at least not yet. Your orders are to stand down and resume your studies at Carnazon. You've already missed a week of classes, and although I've spoken to your professors, you cannot neglect your schooling."

He ran a hand down his beard-stubbled cheek; apparently he had been too busy to shave for several days. "We can't live on the edge forever," he concluded at last, "expecting a war that may never come. The remaining preparations are for the professional soldiers. You two have been profoundly useful already, and you have my respect for what you've done. You've made it back just in time for the Spring Equinox Festival this weekend, so be sure to enjoy the celebration. Dismissed."

Cammie was almost glowing as the two of them made their way from Mazaren Fortress across town to Carnazon. It was good to be appreciated. She had expected Eza to react a little more strongly to Colonel Ennazar's praise, so she poked him in the ribs, drawing laughter out of him. "You're quiet."

"I'm an Introvertian," he said with a giant smile.

"You're quiet when I expected you to be loud."

"Just distracted."

"By what?" Cammie asked, curious.

"You'll see."

"Oh, no, no," she said, coming around in front of him and slowing. "Are you being sneaky?"

Eza ducked left, and as soon as Cammie moved that way to cover, he went around her to the right. "You'll see!"

"Tell me!" she prodded. "I want to know!"

"You will! Just not right now."

She growled, falling in behind Eza and tickling his sides every few steps. "Tell me. Tell me. Tell me."

Eza sped up, staying a few steps in front of Cammie, who knew she couldn't keep up in a foot race. "Okay," she conceded at last, beginning to huff a bit from Eza's rapid pace. "I'll see eventually."

They were almost to Carnazon by then, so Eza

slowed, saying a farewell to Aleiza, who wheeled off and flew low over the streets and houses toward the Skywing home. What was it that he wanted her to see? "Tell meeeeee," she whined one more time. "Pleeeeeeeease."

"In about two minutes, okay?"

"Noooooooo..."

But she followed Eza into the courtyard, up the staircase to the Harmony barracks, and then to the left and into the third-year dorm, where her mouth fell open.

Around twenty Harmony students were dressed in what appeared to be an attempt at Exclaimovian clothes: bright yellow and red shirts, gaudy pants. Some of them even had makeup, or something like it, painted on their faces. As soon as they saw Cammie they erupted, in unison, into a monologue:

"The glories of this day will last forever! As long as men tell stories and children listen with wide eyes and eager ears, the tales of our renown will last! So come, my men, come and drink with me, and celebrate this day as one celebrates the birth of one's firstborn! For what is today if not our return to life from what had been certain death?"

Cammie watched in disbelief. "That's the end of my favorite play," she said softly, her throat starting to tighten up. "*The Glory of Riekaran.* How –" She stared at Eza. "You did this?"

He nodded. "To make you feel more at home."

Suddenly she was crying, in front of everybody. "I hate you so much," she said, smiling through the tears and punching him repeatedly on the shoulder.

Eza couldn't hold in the laughter at this point. "You do not either."

"How did you know about that scene?"

"You quoted it to me that night you were talking about the theater company."

Cammie wiped her eyes. "So you *memorized the entire thing* and wrote it down and then *had all them memorize it too*? Just to make me happy?"

"That's pretty much it, yeah."

All at once she didn't even care who saw her crying. The feeling of self-consciousness just evaporated. She looked at Eza. "I shouldn't have said I hated you. This is one of the nicest things anyone has ever done for me."

Shanna stepped forward. "If you really want to start a theater company, I'll volunteer."

"Me, too," said Eza.

And then Cammie was crying again, pulling Eza and Shanna both toward her. "We're doing it," she said.

NINE

"I've heard people talking about this Spring Equinox Festival for a couple of weeks now," Cammie said. She and Eza were in the Harmony lounge, early on Saturday morning. Eza was giving Cammie one of her customary foot rubs; he didn't know whether she was actually sore (they had done an awful lot of walking in the past week, after all) or whether she just enjoyed the beauty treatment. Eza wouldn't have been totally surprised if she'd asked him to paint her fingernails too.

"It's really fun," Eza told her. "I don't want to spoil too much of the surprise, but it's very...ah, not Introvertian. There's a parade with loud music –"

"A parade?" Cammie interrupted, her eyes bright. "I love parades!"

"And there's a giant dance in the Reading Square –"

"A quiet dance where everyone has their hands in their pockets?"

Eza smirked. "No. You'll see. And there's all sorts of different food from all over the kingdom –"

"Like what?"

That made Eza laugh. "You really don't like suspense, do you?"

"Nope. I want to know everything right now."

"But surprises are fun."

"They're fun when I'm the one keeping a surprise from other people and they're the ones squirming." She pretended to glare at Eza. "I haven't forgotten last night."

"I hope you never do."

Cammie tilted her head. "What do you mean by that?"

"I mean it was fun to do something so meaningful for you. I enjoyed making you happy." Eza half-smiled; that had brought back a memory that was beautiful and painful at the same time. "My mother used to always say that about me, that I was happiest when I was making other people happy."

"I think that's a really wonderful thing," Cammie said.

"Yeah." But Eza didn't want to talk about his mother; he didn't want to start off sad on the day of the Spring Equinox Festival.

Razan came out of the third-year boys' dorm, pausing just long enough to roll his eyes at Eza and Cammie before heading out of the lounge. A few moments later, Anneka came out of the girls' dorm, deliberately pretending not to notice Cammie or Eza sitting by the windows. As the lounge door closed behind her, Eza could see her strike up a conversation with Razan and then head off down the hall with him.

"So I guess they're friends now," Cammie observed.

"Maybe if they make each other happy, they won't have to make other people miserable."

Cammie giggled. "That's very optimistic."

"If you're done being pampered, let's head down to Broad Avenue. I bet the vendors and the food stalls are set up by now."

Cammie looked down at her feet, which were resting on Eza's knee. "Maybe a few more minutes?"

An hour later they were leaving Carnazon's south gate. The streets were...*crowded* wasn't the right word, Eza thought, because all the roads were so wide that people were never shoulder to shoulder even if there were thousands of them. The Spring Equinox Festival, and the Fall Equinox Festival that accompanied it, were the two times of the year when Introvertians suspended their normal aversion to large crowds and decided to join each other in celebration. The summer solstice didn't have its own festival, because it was in the middle of the harvest season, and the winter solstice didn't either, partly because of the cold weather and partly because it fell so close to the Day of Lights, when Introvertians gathered with their families to exchange gifts. Abruptly he realized he should have been telling Cammie all of this rather than just thinking it to itself, but he looked over at her as they turned onto Broad Avenue, and her split-colored eyes were wider than he'd ever seen them.

Eza had heard that Tranquility was home to over three hundred thousand people, and on a day like today he believed it. Broad Avenue was sixty feet wide, with wagons and booths set up on both sides selling art, crafts, home decorations, fruit, baked sweets, and dozens of other things. As far as Eza could see, the whole road was an ocean of people, laughing and playing and joking and enjoying the brilliant spring morning.

"I want to do everything," Cammie murmured, looking excitedly around. "All at the same time."

"Here," Eza said, steering her toward one of the nearby booths. "This is a game I loved when I was younger. If you can knock all the bottles down, you win a stuffed animal."

"Look at the stuffed kitten!" squealed Cammie. "It's *so cute*!"

"Try and win it," Eza encouraged her. "Here. I brought almost all of my money from home. Today would be a great day to use it all."

Eza passed a few coins to the man at the booth, who gave a ball to Cammie. She held it in her hand, closed one eye to aim, and threw the ball clear over the top of the booth, narrowly missing the window of the shop behind. Eza nearly fell over laughing as the booth-keeper hustled around to retrieve the ball. "Don't make fun,"

Cammie said, sounding disappointed. "I wanted that cat."

"I'll get it for you."

"Really?"

The booth-keeper was back by now, so Eza handed over some more coins. The ball was light and the bottles were weighted; that was the trick to the game. The only way to knock them all over was to hit right between those two on the bottom, and to get the middle one hard enough that it bounced into the one on the outside...

He rubbed his thumb on the side of the ball, then cocked back and flung it as hard as he could. *Crash!* Just like he'd planned, all six bottles fell to the ground and the booth-keeper gave him the stuffed kitten with a smile.

"Here," Eza said, giving the kitten to Cammie.

She wrapped both arms around it and hugged it tightly, a childlike smile on her face. "Thank you."

Eza had never imagined her as the stuffed animal type, but there she was, beaming with joy. That brought a smile to his own face. *You're happiest when you're making other people happy...*

Especially Cammie.

"Are you hungry?" he asked. "I see cinnamon buns over there..."

"I want ice cream," Cammie interjected, her eyes wandering to a nearby stall where a vendor was churning a bucket.

"For breakfast?"

"For breakfast." She tilted her head at Eza. "Please?"

"Of course. Whatever you want."

So they had ice cream, and then Cammie bought a beautiful knit blouse that she put on immediately over her normal clothes. He'd found her weakness, Eza thought: street festivals. After an hour they'd only made it two blocks, because Cammie wanted to sample every food and browse every stall and admire every piece of art. Eza didn't mind, of course; he wasn't in a hurry, and it was fun for him to watch Cammie enjoying something she had obviously not expected Introvertians to be capable of doing.

Eza hadn't been quite accurate when he said there was "a dance" in the Reading Square; there were actually three. One was at noon, one at three after the parade had passed, and one at six. There were far too many people for all of them to get into the Reading Square at once, anyway. It was almost noon now, so he hustled Cammie the last block to the Reading Square so they could be there before the music began. He knew she'd love to see this part.

Four different bandstands were set up at the corners of the square, carefully built from curved stones in a way that would best project the music. Even so, the square was too large for the music to be heard from one end to the other, so the four bands each did their own thing, and there was a small area in the middle where none of them could be heard clearly. Eza's favorite band from previous years was The Explorers, who were supposed to perform on the southwest corner of the square. Eza led Cammie in that direction, and in a few moments The Explorers had launched into an upbeat folksy song called "Summer Melody."

Cammie looked expectantly at Eza. "You dragged me all this way. Are you going to dance?"

"Are you going to join me?"

"I don't know any Introvertian dances."

"Here, follow me." Eza showed her the movements of a trot-step he had learned many years ago, and Cammie picked it up almost immediately. Of course, he thought; she had probably done a lot of dancing and choreography for the plays she'd been in. Eza didn't know which of them had the bigger smile as they whirled around each other.

Eza showed her a shuffle-step for the next song, another quick dance, and again Cammie mastered it in seconds. By the end of the song she was putting her own special twists on it, adding a few extra movements that weren't in the original. "That's nice," Eza told her.

Then the song was over, and as the crowd's applause

died down, the band launched into a slower song, a ballad Eza had always loved called "A Midnight Prayer." It was a waltz step, and all around Eza, people paired off, taking hold of each other and walking through the steps of the dance.

Eza and Cammie stared at each other for several long moments. Finally Eza held out his hand. Cammie looked down at it, then back at him with an enormous smile. "Follow me," he said. Cammie put her glasses up on top of her head, a giant smile on her face, and then she wrapped her fingers around his.

He pulled her close, his right hand on the small of her back and his left on her right shoulder. Her arms were draped over his shoulders and her one blue and one brown eye locked on his as Eza led them through the steps of the dance. "Relax," Cammie urged him softly. "You're tense. Don't think so hard about the steps. Just...feel it."

Eza hadn't realized how tight his muscles were, but he took a long breath out and did his best to loosen up. He cleared his mind, focusing on the smile-wrinkles around Cammie's split-colored eyes, on the graceful moves of her body as she followed him, on the gentle warmth of her breath against his neck. This was...*fun*. Eza found himself smiling as well, and he and Cammie glided across their little patch of the Reading Square while the music played around them.

At last the waltz ended, and Eza dropped his hands from Cammie's shoulder and back, but Cammie stayed where she was, her arms gently wrapped around the back of Eza's neck. They stood, motionless, while the band launched into another fast song and the people around started trot-stepping. "Let's not stop," Cammie said quietly.

Eza moved his hands back into place and they went right back to waltzing. All his attention was on Cammie's eyes, but even out of the corner of his vision he could see people looking strangely at him – and he couldn't possibly care. He'd often heard the phrase "she's just singing her own song" used to describe people who were unique, and that was Cammie alright; her entire life in Introvertia was her singing her own song, so if she was waltzing while everyone else was trotting, there was nothing to do but shrug and enjoy it.

After two more songs Cammie at last let go. "That was really fun," she said. "Thank you."

"Thank *you,*" he said. "I never imagined myself dancing in public."

"You were a great leader," she assured him.

"Cammaina Ravenwood, did you just compliment me?"

"No," she said quickly. "I was...flattering you so

you'd be more excited about joining my theater company."

Eza laughed so hard it hurt. "Very well, madam. I accept your flattery."

"Can we sit down somewhere, though?" Cammie asked. "We've been on our feet all morning."

"Sure. My house is only fifteen minutes that way. You could catch a nap before the parade, if you wanted."

"No, no." Cammie's gaze wandered across the Reading Square, where people were still dancing and singing along. "I like the crowds."

So they found an unoccupied bench near the palace, their backs to the Rapidly Flowing River as it burbled and gushed its way to the Great Sea. Eza didn't know how long they rested there, but eventually his stomach began to rumble. "Do you mind if we go get lunch?" he asked.

"I'm hungry, too. It turns out ice cream isn't a great breakfast after all."

Eza led them out the other side of the Reading Square. He hadn't seen his favorite stall on the eastern side of Broad Avenue, and he was hoping it was on the stretch between the Reading Square and the Music Square. His eyes scanned the vendors, hoping to spot –

Yes, *there* it was. "Okay," he told Cammie, "Here's the thing. This place is *amazing*. I don't know what these people do in between equinox festivals, but if they had a restaurant here in town, I would spend *all my money* there." He reconsidered that. "Okay, all the money I didn't spend at Cappel's."

"That's quite the buildup," she told him. "It had better be good."

"Decide for yourself."

Eza could hardly contain his excitement as he approached the stall. "Two Rushwind rolls, please." Rushwind was the second largest city in Introvertia, nestled in the southwest corner right where the Rapidly Flowing River left the Cloudscraper Mountains. Eza had no idea how the people who kept the stall had moved all that meat from Rushwind to Tranquility while it was still marinating, but he was glad they had.

"What am I holding?" Cammie asked a few moments later.

"This is a Rushwind roll. It's kenava meat, marinated for three days, fire-grilled, and put inside this fresh-baked bread. Just smell it."

"I don't want to smell it. I want to eat it."

"Then let's go!" Eza said. He and Cammie began annihilating their sandwiches.

"Okay," Cammie said when her roll was gone. "I don't always trust your taste buds, but *that* was worth it."

They strolled down toward the Music Square, then lazily made their way back. By now it was nearly time for the parade. Broad Avenue had begun to clear off, the huge crowds making their way to the sidewalks so the floats and performers could pass unobstructed. Eza and Cammie sat on the edge of the street, Introvertians pressed tightly around them, and before long they could hear the music of the parade coming.

The first float was a horse-pulled wagon with small children inside, representatives of the Introvertian Kindness League, who threw paper-wrapped sweets into the crowd. One landed in Eza's lap, and he handed it to a boy next to him. After that was a float of musicians, followed by some dancers who twisted and whirled. Group after group came by, but Eza spent more time watching Cammie than he did the parade. The look of rapt fascination on her face was magnetic to him; she was drinking up the parade, and the cheering and shouting of the crowd, like it was nourishing her soul. At one point she caught him watching and blocked her face with her hand for a moment, then looked back at him with a smile as if to say she didn't care after all.

For an hour the floats drifted past, the musicians and singers and performers and candy-throwers and contest winners and army companies. By the end Cammie was resting her elbows on her knees and her chin in her hands, looking for all the world like a giant kid, obviously loving every second of it. When the last float had gone, off toward the Music Square, Cammie stared wistfully after it. "That was amazing," she said distantly.

"I thought you'd like it."

She stood up, stretching herself like she always did right after waking up. "This is the best day I've had in...well, that I can remember."

"It's only two in the afternoon," Eza said.

"Huh. Maybe we should head to your house for that nap after all, then."

"Let's go," Eza agreed, extending his arm to show the way.

It was the best day he could remember, too.

TEN

Cammie and Eza spent Saturday night at Eza's house, the way they usually did on the weekends. In hindsight, Cammie realized, she should have figured out that Eza was up to something the night before, when he had taken them to Carnazon on a Friday instead of directly to his own house, which was closer anyway. But they'd been out on the road for a week before that, and she hadn't been thinking about days of the week at the time. He'd pulled a good one with that whole *Glory of Riekeran* thing, she knew, and she'd have to find a way to get him back somehow.

She always slept better at Eza's house, too, so she was still solidly in bed when a knock sounded on the front door at around nine the next morning. Immediately she heard movement from Eza's room next door, followed by the sound of his feet on the balcony and then on the steps.

The house was built very solidly of stone, including the interior walls, so Cammie couldn't even hear a muffled conversation, but Eza's footsteps sounded very excited as he leaped up the stairs and then threw her door open. "We've been summoned to the palace again."

Cammie pulled the covers over her head.

"We can't keep the king and queen waiting," Eza said, the sound of his voice getting closer.

"Whatever you're thinking about doing, it's very important that you don't," she warned.

But then Eza was jumping on the bed, bouncing Cammie up and down, his giggles mixing with Cammie's panicked yelps. The feather-filled mattress heaved like a ship on rough seas, and Cammie pitched herself halfway out of the bed before Eza accidentally landed on her. "Alright," she said, looking up at him from the ground with her legs still on the bed. "I'm up."

"Let's go, then!"

Without her customary hour to get ready, Cammie had left her hair mostly down, and as with her last summons to the palace, she opted for a forest green shirt with gray pants. She knew the king and queen probably wouldn't judge her for her clothing, but it was important to her to show that she wanted to fit in. In minutes she and Eza were trekking through the Music Square, which was already alive with melodies this early on a Sunday morning, and then into the Reading Square and through the palace doors.

Immediately Cammie sensed tension in the air as soon as she entered the throne room. One glance at the body language of the assembled generals (and Colonel Ennazar, who was once again present) told her that they'd been debating – maybe even arguing – something important, and had not come to a consensus. That made her nervous; anything that got Introvertians arguing with each other had to be really serious.

King Jazan's face wore a similar look of worry, but his face brightened when he saw Cammie and Eza. "Welcome, Cadets."

"At the king's service," Eza said with a salute.

Cammie kept forgetting that part, so she fumbled her way through a salute and smiled at Queen Annaya.

"Please," the king said, extending his arm toward the side of the throne room. "You may have a seat for a few minutes, and I trust it will become apparent why your presence here is required."

Cammie followed Eza to the seats on the room's left side, the same chairs where the Exclaimovian delegation had been seated just a week and a half ago when they'd threatened a three-front war and everything had changed. "Now, then," King Jazan was saying. "I understand that General Nazoa's plan is a controversial one, so before our final vote, allow me to summarize the benefits and disadvantages of an alliance with the Telravians."

"Telravia?" Cammie mouthed silently to Eza, horrified. She'd heard a lot about the Telravians, much of which had doubtless been made up (Exclaimovians tended to exaggerate, after all), but if even half of it was true, theirs was a deeply unpleasant society where treachery, deception, and dark magic were encouraged. She could not imagine a nation more different than Introvertia – even Exclaimovia had more in common with Introvertia than Telravia did.

"The fact remains that we need an ally," King Jazan continued. "Our front-line soldiers still do not know magic. It will take months if not years to train them all, and even then we will have to completely change our battle tactics. Once our soldiers learn magic and our dragons grow to their normal size, we might be able to stand against three enemies at once. At the moment, though, we simply cannot. Claira and Telravia have been engaged in low-level hostilities for several months now, and I have no doubt that Telravia would welcome assistance in that fight."

He surveyed the room. "At the same time, I am also aware that the values of Telravia are fundamentally incompatible with our own. To be extremely blunt, people like the Telravians are the reason we decided to give up magic in the first place. My great-father several centuries ago decided that we would rather live without magic altogether than risk becoming Telravia."

The king looked at his wife, who gave an encouraging nod. "With that said, we are not talking about joining kingdoms. We are not talking about welcoming Telravian citizens into Introvertia to live among us, or adopting their schools of magic. We simply need help. None of us asked for this war that Exclaimovia threatened. All we want is all we've ever wanted: to be left alone, to enjoy life in the way we think best. Anyone who saw the joy and laughter of the Equinox Festival yesterday knows that we have a beautiful thing here in Introvertia. We have something worth protecting, worth fighting for." King Jazan's face hardened. "And if we are going to fight, we are going to win."

"Yay daddy!" came a small voice from one side of the throne room. A chuckle came from the generals as Jayan, the king's seven-year-old son, ran across the dais and wrapped his arms around his father's legs.

A flustered caretaker appeared momentarily, holding Jayan's twin sister Anya in her arms. "I'm sorry, sire. You know how fast he is..."

"Do not apologize for my son," King Jazan said, scooping Jayan up and smiling at him. "He is strong and fast, and smart, and one day he and his sister will lead the greatest kingdom that exists."

"I love you, daddy," Jayan said, burying his face in the king's neck.

"Now, then," the king continued. "We will take a vote on this alliance. As king, all foreign policy decisions rest with me, though you all know that I have never gone against your counsel. Please indicate at this time whether you approve or oppose an alliance – a military alliance only – with Telravia." He sat on the throne, playing with his son while the generals decided how they wanted to vote.

Cammie rapidly counted up the votes, noticing that Colonel Ennazar had kept his hands down. Maybe he didn't get a say because he wasn't a high enough rank. "I think they're tied," she whispered to Eza. "What does that mean?"

"It means the king has to break the tie."

"What do you think he's going to choose?"

"I don't know."

"But – surely you won't ally with *Telravia,* right? They're –"

But King Jazan was standing again, sending his son to run back off toward the caretaker. "This is the first time I can recall your counsel being split," he said. "And that does not make my task any easier. I would rather we speak as one voice, as we did the last time we gathered. But something must be done, and I trust I have made my position clear. As I must break the deadlock, my decision is for an alliance with the Telravians." Distaste was clearly visible on his face. "With an eye toward terminating the alliance as soon as strategic considerations allow."

In Exclaimovia such a decision would have been met with loud protests from all who had opposed, but here, to Cammie's surprise, there was not so much as a murmur. It seemed as if they were all, regardless of whether they had approved or dissented, determined to move forward together in unity. "Which brings us to the matter of Cadet Skywing and Cadet Ravenwood," the king said. "I believe the Telravians will readily agree to an alliance, but just in case they require further persuasion, they will likely be impressed by magical ability. My preference would be to send Colonel Ennazar, but we cannot permit him to leave for the ten to fourteen days that it will take you to travel to Telravia and back. His presence here is required to continue training our cadets in magic and to coordinate our defense. You two cadets must go as our magical representatives."

"We have to impress them with our spellcasting ability?" Cammie repeated.

"Possibly. I have it on good word that their border fort of Desolation Peak is built on a magical node just inside their territory. We will arrange for the meeting to take place there. If you should be required to demonstrate your prowess, the presence of the node will help you. You will travel with two companies of soldiers, including a wing of dragon-companions. One of our senior diplomats, Ambassador Gezana, will be accompanying you as well." The king motioned to a woman about forty years old, with shoulder-length brown hair and a stern face. "She will be negotiating the terms of the alliance, but there is a chance the Telravians will insist on dealing specifically with you two, as the most advanced spellcasters in the group. You will repeat only the instructions that Ambassador Gezana tells you, and it goes without saying that our dragons are not for sale or trade under any circumstances."

"Yes, Your Highness," Cammie and Eza chorused.

"I will notify your professors that you will be missing another week or two of class, and I will have the royal scribes give you some reading material about Telravia's history and culture. The more prepared you are, the better off we will all be."

"Whatever the king requires," Eza said.

"Yes, that," echoed Cammie.

"Report to Mazaren Fortress tomorrow morning by nine. Colonel Camara and Ambassador Gezana will be awaiting you."

Eza, with two books in his hands, led Cammie out the palace doors and into the Reading Square. "I suppose we're going to have a busy day before we leave tomorrow," observed Cammie.

"Busy?" Eza asked. "All we have to do is read."

"Not exactly. You have to do all my laundry."

Cammie watched slow recognition dawn on his face as he remembered the terms of their magical duel from before they'd left on Colonel Ennazar's mission. "No, no," Eza protested. "We *clearly* agreed that the loser had to do the winner's laundry *next week*. It didn't say *any future week of the winner's choosing*. You didn't enforce the deal the next week, so you missed your chance."

"Clearly incorrect," Cammie said, pushing up her glasses. "It wasn't that you would do my laundry *during* the next week. You were to do my laundry *from* the next week, meaning from the Monday after we made the deal until today, the entire *next week* after the deal was made."

"Wrong," Eza said with a chuckle. "The specific wording was that I would *do* your laundry next week. The laundry was not *done* during the required time frame, so the offer expires."

"That just means you failed to hold up your end of the deal!"

"You never gave me your laundry!"

"How about if we go double or nothing," Cammie asked. She didn't really care who washed the clothes; she just loved teasing Eza.

"How about we do it together," suggested Eza instead.

"That sounds fine. But if you turn any of my red shirts pink..." She wagged a warning finger at him.

"I'll make sure to do that."

"HEY!"

"I mean...not to do that," Eza corrected mischievously.

"On second thought, maybe I'll just do it all myself."

ELEVEN

Monday morning brought Eza and Cammie to Mazaren Fortress once more. Eza had to admit that the sight of two companies of Introvertian soldiers, with sixty dragons soaring overhead, took his breath away. Aleiza immediately flew up to join the other dragons, which amused Eza greatly because she was so huge compared to the rest of them. "Cadet Skywing!" a voice said from behind him, and Eza snapped to attention, turning to see an older officer, about fifty, with graying hair. "Captain Grenalla. Pleasure to meet you, Cadet. I've heard much about you."

"The pleasure is mine, sir! Are you any relation to the Academy professor?"

"She's my niece, yes." The captain smiled. "Is she interesting?"

"She's one of my favorite professors, sir. I love the stories she tells from her Ranger days."

"I'll pass that on to her. Let's move out!"

On horseback once again, Eza filed in near the front of the formation as the two companies marched out through the north gate of Mazaren Fortress and up the wide, paved highway that led north toward Resolve. From Resolve it would be a short trip up and around the southeastern foothills of the Cloudscrapers and then into Telravian territory and their border fortress of Desolation Peak.

Who calls a place Desolation Peak? Eza thought to himself. *Seriously*.

Cammie was riding next to him, so he looked over at her. "Do you know much about Telravia?"

"I've heard stories," she said. "I've heard they're ruled by a council of seven of the most powerful sorcerers in the nation, and the only way to get a seat on the council is to kill one of the seven and take their place."

"I've heard that, too, so it's probably true. We had to study Telravia in History class, but they're not exactly known for being open to outsiders, and we like to keep to ourselves anyway, so a lot of things in the textbook were described as being hearsay or secondhand rumors."

"Yeah, same." Cammie shuddered. "I heard they believe the best way to honor the dead is to bring them back with evil magic and have them fight for Telravia."

"So they literally have an army of the dead?"

"If the rumors are true." She took a deep breath of clear morning air. "I've heard worse, too."

"I'm going to wait until I can see for myself," Eza declared. "You know how those stories go. They get bigger and crazier every time a new person tells them."

"Since we have time," Cammie said, pulling some

papers out of her backpack and passing them to Eza, "why don't you start memorizing your lines?"

"My lines?" repeated Eza, unfolding the papers and glancing over them. "This is a play?"

"Not a whole play. More like a skit. Just a little something for you and me and Shanna to perform to get the theater company started."

"Whenever we finally have more than a day back at Carnazon." Eza studied the script. "This is very good," he said. "Is it another one you memorized back in Exclaimovia?"

"No. I wrote this one."

Eza gaped at her. "What? When?"

"You remember how I was really tired yesterday morning and didn't get out of bed?"

"Yes..."

"I was up until three in the morning."

"Ouch. I'm sorry for jumping on your bed, then."

Cammie giggled. "Don't apologize. That was funny."

It took two full days for the companies to arrive at Resolve, and during that time Eza had memorized the entire script – not just his own lines, but Cammie's and Shanna's as well. "It's a shame we don't have a third person," Eza observed. "We could perform this thing for the soldiers."

"You've never seen a single actress play two people?"

Cammie asked.

"No...how?"

"Different clothes and a different voice," Cammie said, as if it should be obvious. "I'd play my own part and Shanna's. When I have to switch to Shanna, I'll put on a scarf and use a higher voice."

"You brought that scarf I got you at the Equinox Festival?"

Cammie dug deep in her bag and produced it. "I hear it gets cold in the north this time of year."

"Well, look at you, being prepared for anything."

"It's the essence of the performing arts," sniffed Cammie with an air of grandeur.

Resolve had a fortress similar to Mazaren and Carnazon, but smaller, part of the old string of border fortresses that Introvertia hadn't needed in several hundred years. Without evil wizards stirring up trouble with Introvertia's neighbors, the kingdom had been able to go back to the isolationist foreign policy that had always been their preferred way of doing things. As long as Introvertia kept its hands to itself, so to speak, the other kingdoms had seemed content to ignore it.

The soldiers were camped in the fortress' courtyard, scattered around several dozen different fires and talking quietly among themselves. One fire was unlit close to Cammie, and she blasted it with a fireball that made it roar immediately to life. Heads turned, and Cammie put her hands triumphantly in the air while Eza tried not to cringe. "Introvertians! If you are a lover of the arts, come to me! We will be putting on a play for your entertainment!"

There was scattered laughter around the camp until the soldiers realized she was serious, and a crowd began to gather. Cammie sprayed a little water on the fire so it died down enough for people on the other side to see her and Eza. "The...uh..." She leaned to Eza. "We don't have a name."

Eza looked at her blank-faced. "I've never named a theater company before."

"The company who is currently but will not forever be without a name," Cammie shouted with a flourish, "proudly presents to you *A Dream of Spring* by Cammaina Ravenwood." She gave a curtsy. "That's me."

By now more than half the soldiers had surrounded them, and more were on the way. This was, after all, the most interesting thing happening in the fortress at the moment, and probably in the whole city of Resolve. "Be sure to be loud," Cammie told him. "Don't talk to me. Talk to the person furthest away from you. And use big gestures." She thought for a moment. "Actually there's a lot I haven't taught you, now that I think about it. Just do your best."

That wasn't exactly a boost of confidence, Eza thought, but he gave it his everything, proclaiming his lines and strutting and trying to feed off the energy he felt Cammie giving him. It wasn't that different from dancing with her, he suddenly realized sometime in the middle of scene two. All his attention was on her, watching her exaggerated motions and reflecting them with his own body, matching the rising and lowering tone and volume of her voice. This...was *fun*.

The climax of the play was when Eza's character, Sazara, saw a flower and realized that spring was coming and winter was over. Privately, Eza didn't consider that an exciting ending, but when that part of the play came, he gave it all he had. Spotting an imaginary flower on the ground, he opened his mouth and crouched by it like it was a chest full of gold and treasure, cupping his hands around it as he looked up at Cammie. "Spring is here," he said, as loudly and tenderly as he could manage. "Winter is over."

"We made it," Cammie said.

That was what the script called for her to say, but Eza took it differently: they'd made it to the end of the play, and he had loved it. The script also called for him to wrap her in a hug, and he put his own spin on that, lifting her off the ground (she was light, but still an inch taller than him) and twirling her around before setting her back down. The wonder and joy on her face were genuine, and they locked eyes for several seconds before turning and bowing to the crowd.

Eza had expected them to grudgingly tolerate it, and was totally unprepared for the thunder of applause that greeted him. He looked at Cammie, obviously surprised. "Congratulations," he told her. "You're a playwright now."

"You did great," she assured him.

"I want more."

She turned to face him again, smiling uncontrollably. "Really?"

"Really."

Cammie smiled at him. "I can't wait to get back to Tranquility."

Before that happened, though, there was the reason they had come north in the first place. The horses left Resolve early the next morning, and Cammie had her scarf wrapped around her neck. It was thirty miles from Resolve to Desolation Peak, which would put the Introvertians there by mid-afternoon. Cammie was really hoping the negotiations were brief and they were able to head back home the same day, even if it meant traveling through the night. The thought of spending the night in Telravia did *not* make her happy at all.

"Are you alright?" Eza asked at one point. "You've been quiet for about two hours now. I'm really worried."

She laughed. "Shut up."

Eza feigned surprise. "An Exclaimovian telling an Introvertian to be quiet? Now I've seen everything."

"I don't mean be quiet. I mean shut up."

"Of course. My mistake."

But Cammie kept staring at him, and eventually Eza looked back over at her. "Something up?" he asked her.

"You know me really well."

Eza smiled. "I'd like to think so."

"No, I mean you didn't get offended when I told you to shut up twice. You know when I'm joking."

"I'd be lying if I said I liked it, but yeah, I know how you talk. I know when say you hate me you don't really mean you hate me."

Cammie could feel her cheeks turning red. "Ah, that's...true..."

Eza faced forward again, unable to hide his triumphant grin. "I love making you speechless."

Cammie looked down at her horse, then back at Eza. "I hate you."

"No, you don't."

There was a long pause. "No," she admitted with a wide smile. "I don't."

The weather got colder as they rounded the

Cloudscraper Mountains and headed northwest toward Telravia. The sky, which had been its usual brilliant blue when they left Introvertia, had turned cloudy as soon as they'd passed the mountains. "Great," Cammie said. "This place even *looks* gloomy."

Desolation Peak didn't do anything to help her mood either. The fortress was built into the side of a mountain, and it had eighteen tall towers that rose to points as if trying to pierce the sky. For the first few hours it was on the horizon, it looked like a normal if vaguely threatening fortress. It wasn't until they turned to enter the front gates that Cammie saw the whole thing looked like a giant spiked skull.

"Who builds a fort shaped like a skull?" she whispered to Eza.

"Probably not the good guys."

The two hundred Introvertians and their sixty dragons passed through the gates and halted in the outer yard. Ambassador Gezana stood near Cammie and Eza; if she was thinking anything, she didn't share it with them. At last a door opened in the central keep and a handful of Telravians came out. Cammie's nose wrinkled in visible distaste. They were pale, their skin too tight as if it had been stretched over a frame that was supposed to look like a person but didn't quite get there. Their eyes were dark, but not bright-dark like Queen Annaya's.

They were dead-dark. Cammie didn't know exactly what she meant by that, only that the effect was *extremely* disgusting to her.

But she also knew couldn't judge them on appearances, so she forced herself to be calm. In surprise she found her hand holding tightly onto Eza's, but she didn't let go, and neither did he. One of the Telravians descended the steps into the outer yard and spoke in a voice that sounded like wind through a graveyard.

"Introvertians..." hissed the man or possibly woman. "We are extremely satisfied that you have come."

"The pleasure is entirely ours," said Ambassador Gezana, bowing. "I am Terari Gezana, senior diplomat of the Kingdom of Introvertia. These are Ezalen Skywing and Cammaina Ravenwood, my assistants."

The Telravian peered at Cammie, a stare which seemed to pass through her and which caused the hair on the back of her neck to stand up. "This one is not from among you," the wind-voice declared.

"She is one of ours now," Ambassador Gezana said. "To whom do I have the pleasure of speaking?"

"I am the Voice of the Seven."

Ambassador Gezana shifted uneasily. "Exalted Voice, we bring to you an offer of a military alliance. We know you have been under assault from the Clairans for –"

"We accept."

Ambassador Gezana hesitated. "Excuse me?"

"We accept your offer of alliance," the Voice wheezed. "Your might will be added to our own, and together we will defeat the Clairans."

"As well as the Esterians and the Exclaimovians," Ambassador Gezana added. "We are under threat from all three kingdoms."

"And all three will crumble before our wrath," the Voice said, and Cammie shivered with her entire body.

A deafening screech pierced the outer yard, and a monstrous horror descended from the mountains. It looked like a skeletal dragon, shards of flesh dangling from its wings and moldy eyes in its nearly empty sockets. Cammie felt like she was going to throw up, and squeezed Eza's hand so hard she knew it had to be hurting him.

"Tell us," the Voice said softly. "Are there any among you who do magic?"

"I do," Cammie said, stepping forward. Immediately she was regretting it – she'd blurted without thinking, as usual –

The Voice examined her with its blank eyes, and Cammie had to fight with all her strength not to reach out and punch it. "Intriguing. Why are you among these ones?"

Cammie said nothing.

"You will demonstrate your magic for us," the Voice ordered.

Cammie had never liked being told what to do, especially not by this *thing*. The skeletal dragon had landed and was standing about fifty feet away by the stairs up to the citadel. Cammie could feel the tingling from the nexus node, but she held the power in, building the power within her but not letting it go.

She was disgusted, didn't want to be here in this horrible place with these horrible people and their horrible creatures. Why had Introvertia allied with them? Cammie let the anger pile up in her, stoked it as it slowly turned to fury, and just as her emotions were on the ragged edge –

"Well?" the Voice goaded.

Cammie screamed and lightning seared out of her hands, striking the skeletal dragon in hundreds of places across its wings and head and body. Its dying screech echoed off the mountains and the stone walls of the citadel, and dozens of Introvertian soldiers threw their hands over their ears. Almost before Cammie's eyes could see what had happened, the dragon's bones had melted and its twisted body lay smoking on the ground.

Total silence fell on the yard, and Cammie suddenly wondered if she had just started a war.

But the Voice was smiling – a look even more

disgusting than its normal face, as skin peeled back from its lips and exposed gray teeth. Then it began to laugh. Cammie's hand found Eza's again and she heard his knuckles crack as she tightened her grip.

"Impressive," the Voice said. "You will make worthy allies. Of that, the Seven have no doubt. Which of you will be remaining here as our military liaison?"

"I will," Ambassador Gezana said in a tone that said she'd rather be executed on the spot.

"And which of your dragons will you be leaving here as recompense for the one of ours that was just destroyed?"

Cammie's eyes got wide. If they wanted to pick one, they would doubtless pick Aleiza, who was the largest by far –

"Our dragons are not for sale or trade under any circumstances," Ambassador Gezana said.

"Surely you –"

"*Any,*" the ambassador interrupted sternly, "circumstances. This is not negotiable."

Cammie's eyebrows raised in surprise. She'd only ever heard one or two Introvertians interrupt someone else. Anything that got an Introvertian *that* mad was serious business.

The Voice merely nodded. "We will notify you of our upcoming military campaigns and you will cooperate."

"If this concludes our business," Ambassador Gezana said, "then I will send my soldiers on their way."

The Voice bowed. "We will see you on the battlefield, where the glories of Telravia and Introvertia will live throughout the ages."

"Company, march!" shouted Captain Grenalla, obviously intending that they not spend a single moment longer than necessary in Telravia. The soldiers mounted their horses, which had somehow not bolted when the skeletal dragon arrived, and set a fast gallop southeast.

"Do you think Ambassador Gezana will be okay?" Cammie said to Eza as quietly as she could.

"I don't think they'll harm her. They seemed to need this alliance as badly as we do. Don't forget they've been fighting Claira and Esteria by themselves for...oh, years now, I think, if not decades."

Cammie watched his face for a few moments. "Do you believe this is really the right thing?"

She knew his thinking face. He was turning words over in his head to make sure the right ones came out. He'd told her once that Introvertians liked to craft ideas in their minds and only share the idea once it was fully formed. Cammie preferred to think out loud and figure out as she was talking exactly what she was trying to say.

"I think," he said at last, "that circumstances outside our control forced us to make a really difficult decision."

"Do you think this alliance was the *right* decision?" she pressed.

Eza was quiet for a long time. "No," he said. "But what other choice did we have? Fight a three-front war and get thousands of Introvertians killed? Any decision would have been the wrong one."

"I just hope they keep that evil magic out of Introvertia. And Exclaimovia too for that matter."

"Me too."

TWELVE

Eza had been wondering whether Captain Grenalla was going to stop them for the night or keep going, and sometime around nine o'clock, with a giant full moon rising to the west and a sky full of stars overhead, he figured he had his answer. They wouldn't be able to make it all the way back to Resolve even if they rode until dawn; it was an eight-hour ride under the best of conditions, and the soldiers were taking it easy on the horses, not wanting one to twist an ankle in the dark. They would, however, be away from Telravia, and apparently Eza and Cammie were not the only ones who wanted to be gone from there.

They had almost reached the furthest spur of the Cloudscrapers, where they would turn southwest toward Resolve, when one of the picket scouts came galloping up to Captain Grenalla at full speed. Eza was a few dozen paces behind them and couldn't hear the words, but in the moonlight he saw the scout point at a patch of thick woods a few hundred yards away across the plain. Captain Grenalla halted the two companies, quickly ordering them to fan out in a defensive formation. Eza motioned to Cammie and both of them dismounted their horses, crouching behind the front lines. Was there going to be a battle? Eza's heart was beating hard. He could sense Cammie looking at him, and he reached out to her, taking her hand like she had taken his earlier.

"What's happening?" she asked.

"I don't know."

In the next second there was distant screaming, and dozens or hundreds of troops came pouring out of the far forest. Eza had no clue how many there were, but fireballs and lightning bolts began blasting across the empty plain between the two sides. The Introvertian dragons, with Aleiza at the front, climbed high into the air and then hurtled down, roaring. Aleiza spewed fire and the other dragons crashed down with talons and fangs. Screams and shouted orders echoed across the battlefield, ending with a cry of, "For Claira!"

"Clairans," Eza and Cammie said at the same time.

"Boop," Cammie said, poking Eza on the nose.

His brain tied itself in knots and he stared at her in confusion. "What?"

"Boop," Cammie repeated, poking Eza's nose again. "It's a thing we did in Exclaimovia. When you say something at the same time as someone else, whoever says *boop* and boops the other one's nose first wins."

Eza felt a slow smile spread across his face. This was the worst possible time to be amused by a silly competition, but he couldn't help himself. "We're doing it now."

"If we both survive whatever's about to happen."

"Yeah. So please do. I'm going to win the boop game."

But magical energy was lancing through the night air now, smashing into the ground behind the Introvertian troops, who were still lying on the ground waiting for the Clairans to get closer. Out of the forest came a screech followed by dark shapes that blotted out the stars. Eza strained his eyes. "Falcons?" he asked. "I heard the Clairans use –"

"Combat falcons, yeah," Cammie said. "Can you tell what's happening?"

Dark shapes were whirling around each other, but Eza couldn't see much of anything against the stars. There was a blast of fire, which must have been Aleiza, and some dragon screams – were they screams of victory or of pain?

"Charge!" Captain Grenalla shouted, and the Introvertian soldiers leaped to their feet as one, surging toward the Clairan troops.

"That means us," Eza said, leaping to his feet and sprinting toward the front lines. He didn't know how he could use his Artomancy to turn the tide of battle, but the Clairans definitely had magic, so he had to do something. If he didn't and something happened to

Cammie...

Something changed inside him, and suddenly he didn't care about himself anymore. All that mattered was keeping Cammie safe. The two of them ran forward, shoulder to shoulder, staying behind the Introvertian lines. The professional soldiers knew how to fight together; he just needed to stay safe and stay out of their way.

"Let's strafe," he said suddenly.

"What?"

Of course. Cammie wasn't a soldier and wouldn't know what that meant. "Fire off a bunch of magic, and then I'm going to rainbow door us across the battlefield. That way when the Clairans shoot back, we'll be gone."

A smile crossed Cammie's face. "I like it."

Bright light, nearly blinding, kept erupting from the Clairan lines as the dragons swooped down and blasted with fire. Lightning and fireballs answered from the ground, shooting up into the star-filled sky. While the Clairans were looking up, Cammie opened fire.

Five fireballs left her hands quickly, adding to the destruction poured out by the dragons, and then a shimmering multicolored door opened beside her. She and Eza stepped through together, emerging sixty feet away, behind the Introvertian archers. Every time a Clairan spellcaster's hands started to glow, five

Introvertian arrows converged on the spot. It seemed to Eza like they were winning –

But then a roar came from the woods – no, forty roars all at once. The Clairans had brought their arctic tigers! The archers pivoted, but it would take an incredibly lucky shot to take down a tiger; the most they could do was hope to slow them down a few steps...

Cammie had noticed the threat, too, and she fired off lightning at the tigers, who spun and came straight for the archers – and for Cammie and Eza behind them. In a flash another rainbow door took them about fifty feet more to the right – dragons were torching the tigers, but some were getting through.

What could Eza do? Gar had said himself that Artomancy wasn't combat magic, but he could do light, and heat, and growth...

Growth...

Eza pushed out hard, and tendrils of grass burst up from the ground, wrapping up five of the tigers. He reached deep inside, desperate to contain all the tigers he could, but his magic just wasn't strong enough. "Attack those ones!" Eza ordered, hoping Cammie would know what he meant.

She did, and all five of the immobile tigers ignited in a burst of lightning. Quickly Eza took down five more, just steps before they would have been on top of the archers, and those tigers hit the ground – but Cammie staggered to her knees. "I'm okay," she told Eza. "I just need a minute."

Warmth...

Eza moved himself in front of Cammie, making sure any spells or tigers that wanted to get to her had to come through him first. Most of the tigers were down now, but even one was enough to kill or maul all the Introvertians within swiping distance. Eza had never tried this, never even *thought* of trying this, but he reached deep inside the tiger with warmth energy. He could feel it superheating, could feel its insides turning to steam, and then it burst into flame, skin and fur igniting. The tiger roared in pain and terror, and ran – thankfully back into the woods; if it had run around the Introvertian lines, it could have caused real chaos –

But he could feel a kind of hollow emptiness inside him; that spell had taken almost all of his energy, and he didn't dare try it again. If both he and Cammie ended up exhausted, and Eza couldn't keep them safe if danger came...

Aleiza hurtled just inches over his head, banking toward the remaining tigers, who were hesitating now, unsure whether to keep charging. A ferocious fire-strafing from Aleiza made the choice for them, and even from fifty yards away Eza could smell tiger flesh burning.

In his obsession with the tigers, Eza hadn't noticed that the sounds of battle were getting further away. Not many Clairans were left alive, and the few that remained looked as if they'd decided to withdraw.

Cammie looked up from the ground. "Thanks for keeping me safe, Eza."

"You're welcome."

He offered a hand to help her up, and she took it, climbing to her feet. There in the moonglow they stared at each other, the light bright on Cammie's dark hair, sparkling off her split-colored eyes and glasses. It seemed like there was something she wanted to say to Eza, but whatever it was, she settled for a smile and a squeeze of his hand. *Just when I think I'm starting to understand her,* he thought, grinning to himself. "Come on. Let's go find Captain Grenalla."

The two of them jogged across the battlefield. The Introvertians had pursued the Clairans well into the forest. The Clairans were not running away, like Eza had thought; even in the face of certain defeat, they'd merely retreated into the woods to form a battle line, but so many had died that there was no way they could resist the Introvertians. In a matter of minutes silence had fallen.

None of the Clairans had surrendered. Every last one

of them had thrown himself or herself into the battle, preferring to die by an Introvertian sword than be taken alive. Somehow in the dark Eza found Captain Grenalla, who was still atop his horse, although his face and clothes and scana were covered in blood.

"I heard them say *death before* dishonor," the captain said quietly, as if he couldn't believe what had just happened. "I thought it was an expression. I didn't expect..." He ran his hand through his hair, which was probably a mistake, because it smeared blood all across his head. Somehow he didn't seem to notice.

One of his junior officers came galloping up. "We lost twenty-eight dead, sir. And thirty-eight wounded."

"The Clairans?"

"We counted ninety-nine dead."

"None surrendered?" Captain Grenalla asked in disbelief.

"No, sir. We don't know if that means there's still one out in the woods somewhere, or if he escaped back home to tell them what happened."

Eza was still thinking about warmth, so he tried something new. Clearing his mind, he focused on the heat coming from the people around him. There was Cammie, bright and hot as usual, and Captain Grenalla and his horse. Most of the bodies on the ground, Introvertian and Clairan alike, were dead and cooling.

Eza wandered off to his left; he didn't know much about battlefield medicine, only the basic first aid he'd learned in school in case he were injured in the wilderness, but he might be able to help a little if he found someone injured.

It was like he was looking through different eyes, seeing everything in dark blue except for the heat. Trees appeared a slightly lighter blue, and the living soldiers around him as bright yellow or even white. The dead were dark red fading to deep blue-green, and the injured were orange or bright red. In front of him sat a huge hole about eight feet around where something, maybe Cammie's magic, had blown the ground apart. A tree sat on the back side of it, and was now leaning over the hole, half of its roots having been ripped out of the soil. Tucked into the very edge of the hole, as if trying to hide under the destroyed tree, was someone bright white.

Eza blinked a few times, clearing his vision, and then knelt down next to the soldier. The uniform was not Introvertian. Eza had found a living Clairan. Cammie was right behind him, hunched over his shoulder, and Eza could feel the crackle of magic in her hands in case the Clairan lunged at him with a knife.

He didn't know quite what to say, because he'd never taken a prisoner before. "Clairan soldier, you will come with me and report to my company captain."

"Leave," the soldier croaked. It was a girl. Eza breathed some light into his palm, a soft glow so that he could see what he was looking at. The girl didn't look much older than Cammie, and her face was a tangled mask of fear, pain, and loss.

"You're safe," Cammie said, stepping forward.

The girl shook her head. His magical light reflected off tears on her cheeks. "I failed," she said quietly. "Death before dishonor. I survived while all the others died."

"Surviving isn't failure," Cammie reasoned. "You can just go back home and –"

"Don't you see?" the girl cried, and by now several other Introvertians were approaching to see what the commotion was. Eza waved them off, and for some reason they listened, staying back twenty feet with their hands on their swords and bows. "Don't you see?" the girl repeated more quietly. "I can never go home. They were slaughtered, and I lived. There is no greater dishonor."

Claira didn't sound much more appealing than Telravia did, Eza thought. A society that would rather people die in battle than return to their families? That wasn't a good place at all.

Cammie put her hands on her hips. "Well, we're not going to kill you."

"And I don't want to die," the girl said, shaking her head again. "I don't truly want death before dishonor."

"That doesn't mean there's something wrong with you," Eza said.

"No. But it means I can never go home. It's better for everyone to think I died."

Pity and sympathy bubbled up inside Eza. He took a knee next to her, and Cammie did the same right beside him. "I'm Ezalen," he said. "We'll help you however we can."

"I'm Cammie. You can trust Eza."

Finally the girl raised herself to a sitting position. "I'm Denavi. Do with me as you will."

THIRTEEN

Denavi had said nothing, and eaten nothing, for the entire two days it took the lead group of Introvertians to get home. As Captain Mozara had done at the magical node, the companies had split. A hundred uninjured soldiers, with Eza and Cammie and Denavi among them, had made their best speed back to Tranquility, while thirty healthy soldiers stayed behind to bury the dead and help the wounded return.

Everything about Denavi radiated total devastation. Her back was slouched and her shoulders slumped, and she didn't try to cushion the horse's steps, so her head jostled all around. She didn't seem to be looking at anything at all; her eyes were pointed somewhere vaguely near the horizon, and she didn't acknowledge Cammie or Eza when they rode up next to her and tried to start a conversation.

That didn't stop Cammie from trying, of course; she spent hours and hours talking to Denavi, or perhaps talking *at* Denavi. She didn't say anything about their recent missions that would have given away any military secrets, but she covered *just about* everything else, Eza thought.

If Denavi had the slightest interest – or disinterest –

she didn't show it.

The longer she was quiet, the more Eza felt sorry for her. Was she really to be exiled from her society forever, for the crime of surviving a battle? Denavi had sure seemed to think so. But then what would happen to her in Introvertia? Would they interrogate her, find out all they could about Claira, and then kick her out to fend for herself? Yes, King Jazan and Queen Annaya had made Cammie a citizen of Introvertia, but that had really been the only appropriate thing to do for Cammie after she had helped the kingdom in such an important way. Would they do the same for Denavi? Or would they think she was some kind of spy?

The company made quite an entrance to Tranquility at mid-morning, entering by way of Mazaren Fortress and passing within just a few blocks of Eza's house on their way down to the Reading Square and the palace. Some people waved to the soldiers, while others stared in wonder at the stranger in a strange uniform who rode empty-eyed near the front. Children kept running around the convoy, cheering at Eza and Cammie and Denavi. Eza smiled and waved back to the people who greeted him, but the smile was forced. He was thinking about what was going to happen when they reached the palace.

Guards opened the palace doors and Eza and

Cammie followed Captain Grenalla in, with Denavi in tow behind them. They did not head toward the throne room, where Eza had been expecting – but that made sense, didn't it; why would anyone take a prisoner of war to the throne room? Why had they brought her to the palace at all, rather than leaving her in the secure fortress at Mazaren?

They steered Denavi to a long room on the western wall of the palace, where six tall but narrow windows looked out on the Rapidly Flowing River and the edge of the Reading Square. Denavi was given a seat halfway down a rectangular table, with a few guards in the room to keep her company. Eza, Cammie, and Captain Grenalla waited just outside.

General Nazoa arrived a few moments later. Eza didn't know the man well, but he'd asked an insightful question when Colonel Ennazar was first explaining nexus nodes, so Eza hoped he was an intelligent and thoughtful man. "Do you have anything to add to what was written in your dispatches?" the general asked Captain Grenalla. He suddenly noticed Eza and Cammie standing there. "Cadet Skywing. Cadet Ravenwood. What are you doing here?"

Captain Grenalla interjected. "These two are the only ones the prisoner has ever spoken to."

The general clearly had not been expecting that

answer. He looked from Eza to Cammie and then back to Captain Grenalla. "The only ones?" he repeated.

Captain Grenalla nodded.

General Nazoa chewed on the inside of his lip for several seconds. "Very well. They will conduct the interrogation, then."

"Sir?" Eza asked, his eyes widening.

"I'll tell you what to ask. Based on what Captain Grenalla has said, I doubt she would respond well to a general bursting into the room and barking questions at her. Don't you agree?"

"Yes, sir," Eza said, hoping they were both right. "Very clever, sir."

Eza and Cammie were steered toward seats directly across the table from Denavi, and to Eza's shock, Captain Grenalla and General Nazoa stayed in the hallway immediately outside the room, where they could overhear Denavi's answers but not be seen by her. The general had slipped Eza a paper with a few questions on it, and Eza tried to make eye contact with Denavi.

"Hey," he said. "We just have some things to ask you. What's your name?"

He could hardly believe his ears when Denavi actually answered. "Denavi Kiresti."

"And you're a member of the Clairan army?" he asked.

"I was. Dishonor before death. That's me."

Eza showed the paper to Cammie, who asked the next question. "What's your role in the army?"

"I was a healer."

"Like...a battlefield doctor?" Cammie clarified.

"No. Magical healer."

Eza leaned forward. "Healing magic?" he repeated, without meaning to. Great. Now he was blurting things out like Cammie.

"Yes, Ezalen. Healing magic."

"Could you show us how to do that?" he pressed. The question hadn't been on his script, but Cammie had said something about improvisation being the soul of drama, so he went with it.

"Why would I?"

Cammie stood, pushing back her chair so hard it clattered to the ground behind her. "Okay," she said, pushing her glasses up and putting both hands on her hips. "You've spent the last two days feeling sorry for yourself, Denavi, and it's about to end. You say you dishonored yourself, and your people won't take you back. Fine. There's nothing you can do about that." She swooped toward the table, planted both hands on it, and leaned in toward Denavi, who was staring at her with a mixture of doubt and disbelief. Dramatic Cammie was absolutely in her element, thought Eza, as he tried to hide his amusement. "Or is there?" Cammie asked quietly. "What if you could get the honor you want some other way?"

Denavi said nothing, but her dark brown eyes were locked on Cammie.

"Your people may not want you," Cammie continued, "but Introvertia does. They took me, an Exclaimovian. You could find honor here, Denavi. You can help Introvertia and be well respected in this society. Help us stop this war, Denavi. Tell us what you can, and do your part. You can find a new home, right here. I did."

It must have been dusty in the room, Eza decided. That was the reason his eyes were suddenly watering.

Denavi looked up at the spot where the wall met the ceiling, then out at the hallway where General Nazoa and Captain Grenalla were lurking, although she had no way of knowing they were there. "Thank you," she told Cammie.

"So what can you tell us about Claira?" Cammie asked.

Denavi and Cammie talked for hours. Denavi had gone into incredible detail about Clairan society, the Noble Enlightened Warrior philosophy, the organization of the army, their battle tactics, the kinds of magic they used, and dozens of other things that no spy would possibly have told the people she'd been sent to spy on. Eza was sure that General Nazoa's wrist was sore from taking notes, so at one point, when Cammie had gotten Denavi talking about the kinds of music she liked, Eza had wandered off into the hall to see what was happening out there.

Captain Grenalla was gone, but General Nazoa and King Jazan were seated on chairs, with the general writing and the king hunched over and conferring with him. They both looked up when they saw Eza approaching. "Cadet Skywing," said the king approvingly. "Once again you find yourself in the palace."

"At the king's service," Eza said automatically.

"Since you brought it up," the king said with a smile. "You can imagine that I have a predicament regarding our Clairan friend. It isn't entirely clear to me whether she's a prisoner of war or a guest of the kingdom. She certainly seems to have given Cadet Ravenwood quite a bit of valuable information, so it wouldn't do to keep her in a detention cell. However, until we're able to investigate and find out whether she's told the truth or lied to us, it also wouldn't do to let her roam free. If she is some sort of Clairan agent, she could use the opportunity to gather more information about Tranquility."

"Yes, Your Highness," Eza said, not knowing where all this was going.

King Jazan smiled at Eza, a warm fatherly smile that made Eza feel at ease. "You may be the solution," the king told him. "I would like for you to consider taking Miss Kiresti to your home. She would, for the time being, be under house arrest. Your home would be guarded and she would not be allowed to leave. But I believe she'd prefer that to being in a cell. She knows you and she seems to be comfortable with Cadet Ravenwood."

"Cammie has that effect on people," agreed Eza.

King Jazan nodded. "She does. And I'm sure your father will understand. He has been a loyal servant of the kingdom for a number of years."

"Of course, Your Highness."

It took another two hours before Denavi ran out of things to talk about. Cammie could have kept going until nightfall, Eza knew; she'd found someone new to share all her stories with, so she was retelling all the ones she'd told Eza fifteen times already, even though he loved them the fifteenth time as much as he'd loved them the first time. At last Eza was able to get a word in.

"Denavi," he said with a smile. "We've got an extra bedroom in my house. Would you like to stay with me for a few nights?"

"REALLY?" Cammie shouted gleefully, at the same

time Denavi quietly said, "Okay."

A few minutes later the three of them were stepping out into the evening sun and walking toward Eza's house, with a dozen of the king's guards behind them, drawing stares as they made their way through the Reading Square. "We have to be quiet here," Cammie said helpfully. "This is where people read. There's a lot of quiet stuff here in Tranquility."

"I suppose that explains the name of the place," Denavi whispered. "It's kind of nice."

"Noooooo," Cammie told her in horror. "Loud is nice. You want loud."

"I kind of like quiet."

Cammie looked sideways at Eza. "This is all your fault," she whispered.

He laughed and put his hand on her shoulder. "Probably."

Denavi glanced behind them. "Why are there so many soldiers following us?"

Eza knew he had to be direct with her if he wanted her to believe him and Cammie. "The king still doesn't know if he can trust you. He has to verify everything you said before he knows for sure you were telling us the truth. Until then my house will be under guard and you won't be able to leave."

"But you will?" Denavi asked.

"We have to." Eza had to pause while he tried to remember what day of the week it was. "Tomorrow is Friday, I think, so we have to go to class. But after that is the weekend, and we're always home on the weekends."

Denavi didn't answer, looking around at the tall evergreen trees and the gray and brown buildings. The sun was filtering through dancing branches, golden light spilling over the streets. "This place is pretty."

"I'm glad you like it," said Eza.

In minutes they were at the Skywing house. Ezarra was outside, working in the garden as he usually did after getting home from work. Aleiza had flown back home when Eza arrived in the city, but she exploded over the top of the house, winging toward Eza so hard he was worried she would knock him over onto his back. But the dragon pulled up just short of him, nuzzling his neck with her snout and making him squirm and laugh. "You're the best," he told her, rubbing her neck.

"You can talk to dragons?" Denavi asked, her dark eyes wide.

"A lot of Introvertians can. That's our thing." Eza turned to his father. "Dad, this is Denavi Kiresti. She's a Clairan, but she's going to live with us for a while."

Eza's father smiled. "Pleased to meet you, Denavi Kiresti. I'm Ezarra Skywing."

"The pleasure is mine, sir," Denavi said formally,

bowing to him.

Ezarra looked at his son with a smirk. "But if you bring anyone else home, some of you are going to have to share a bedroom."

Denavi had finished her dinner almost before the others had put knife to meat, and stared in embarrassment at her empty plate before working up the courage to ask for seconds. Ezalen got up from the table to serve her more; she kept hearing people call him Eza, so she assumed that was what he preferred to be called. He filled her plate again with a smile, and Denavi couldn't help smiling back.

"I'm glad you're talking now," Cammie told Denavi. "This is way more fun than you being quiet."

"About that," Denavi said seriously. "I suppose I should tell you why I reacted the way I did. Clairans don't know much about Introvertia, except what we hear from others. Our allies in Esteria have spent years telling us that you're untrustworthy, that you're quiet because you're always planning something. They say you tell people one thing and then stab them in the back. And then...just before my company marched out, there was a man who came to Arkiana, telling us all these horrible things. He said you had gotten magic back because you were planning to attack us and conquer us, that you were going to force us all to spend our lives in silence."

"Truly a fate worse than death," Cammie murmured, smirking at Eza.

"But it looks like you changed your mind," Eza pointed out.

Denavi nodded. "Two things did it. The first was Cammie." Cammie beamed with pride, then squealed and hurled herself backward on the couch when Eza poked her in the side. They were cute together, Denavi thought. "Cammie was just so nice to me. She seemed to truly care whether I liked her or not, even when I didn't respond at all. Then I started thinking about how she's an Exclaimovian and she enjoys being here. That was when I began to question what I'd been told."

Denavi smiled; she was a little embarrassed about this part. "The second thing was the children. When we first rode into Tranquility, the children smiled and waved at me." She thought about what to say next. "They just seemed...nice, you know? Innocent. Not like people who were being groomed to hate and destroy all outsiders. They didn't care if I was a stranger. They were going to greet me anyway."

Cammie had apparently forgiven Eza for his tickle attack; the two were sitting shoulder to shoulder, listening to Denavi. "That's a really wonderful story," Eza said. "Thank you for sharing it."

"I hope I'm not wrong about you," Denavi said, brushing her dark hair back. "But you two have been really kind. I think I'll be okay here. I keep remembering what Cammie said, that I could win honor here the same way I could have won it back home, and I hope I get the chance to try soon."

Ezarra appeared at the back door and Eza sprang up from the couch. The two of them carried a large metal basin full of steaming water up the stairs, clanging it off the walls and bumping their own shins every so often. "That's a lot of hot water," Denavi said in surprise.

"When you have a dragon, you get hot water any time you want it," Cammie pointed out.

The two Skywings came back down the stairs. "There's a warm bath ready in your room," Eza said to Denavi. "I know for a fact you haven't bathed in at least two days, and, uh..." He waved his hand in front of his nose.

"EZA!" howled Cammie, trying to cover up her laughter.

But Denavi was laughing too, and it felt *good*. Her friends in Claira had been all business, all about the pursuit of the Noble Enlightened Warrior, but it felt like Eza and Cammie cared about her as a person. Of course, it was too early to say for sure. Maybe Denavi was just experiencing some kind of strange stress-trust from all the sudden changes. But if life in Introvertia felt this way forever, she would be okay with that.

Denavi had to admit that Eza was right; once she got alone in her new bedroom, she could *definitely* smell herself. The hot bath felt nice, and she lingered in the basin for what felt like an hour, massaging off all the grime and letting the warmth relax her muscles. There were several changes of clothes in her room, a bright red shirt and purple pants that must have been Cammie's, and a short-sleeved gray shirt with brown pants that were probably Eza's. She felt drawn to the quiet simplicity of Eza's outfit. The soft cotton felt nice on her skin; Introvertians obviously enjoyed feeling comfortable. Fully refreshed, hoping her bare feet weren't tracking water across the floor, Denavi stepped out of the bedroom.

Ezarra was just coming up the stairs toward his own room, and he stopped with a smile when he saw Denavi. "Was everything alright?"

"Perfect, sir. Thank you." She fought the urge to salute him.

"Please tell me if there's anything else we can do for you. Any friend of Eza's is a friend of mine."

"Thank you, sir," Denavi said again. "How long have Cammie and Eza been together?"

"Oh, they're not courting." In response to Denavi's

blank look, Ezarra clarified, "They're not a romantic couple."

"Hmm," said Denavi, surprised. "They sure act like they're a couple."

"They do, and I think they'd be perfect together. But that's something they'll have to discover for themselves." Ezarra tilted his head, as if he were thinking of a memory from long ago or far away. "Besides, going from friends to more than friends is a big risk. I've seen lots of people drift apart because they were really great friends but weren't right for each other in a courting relationship. Eza has told me he truly cherishes what he has with Cammie, and I know it would break his heart to lose that."

Denavi nodded in understanding. "Do you think he would take the risk of courting?"

"For Cammie? Absolutely. But that's a decision he'll have to make for himself, in his own time." Ezarra chuckled to himself. "Although something tells me if he waits too long, Cammie will help him make it."

From downstairs she could hear Cammie screeching and Eza laughing hysterically; he had probably been winding her up about something and enjoying her reaction.

"Go join them," Ezarra encouraged her. "You're among friends."

This all seemed too incredible to be real, Denavi thought. Two days ago she'd thought her life was over; she'd dishonored herself and would never be accepted back in Claira. Now she had friends and a home in Introvertia. It felt *wrong* somehow, like she shouldn't be allowed to be so happy after failing her nation and herself.

But two hours later, as she padded her way back up the stairs and slipped under the blankets, she couldn't remember her face and sides ever hurting so much from laughter. Exhaustion finally tightened its grip on her, weariness from the match out of Claira, the battle itself, the fast ride to Tranquility, and all the emotions wrapped together. She closed her eyes, and just as she was about to fall asleep, one final thought occurred to her.

Her people had always told her that honor was the most important thing, that there was no greater aspiration in life. But then, her people had also told her that Introvertians were insincere schemers and backstabbers, and that sure looked false. If she'd been lied to her whole life about Introvertians...what else might Claira be wrong about?

FOURTEEN

"I didn't realize how much I'd be looking forward to just a normal day of class," Cammie told Eza as they approached the south gate of Carnazon. "It's been...what, almost two weeks?"

"Almost exactly."

"I wonder what everyone learned while we were gone."

Eza smiled. "Don't worry. I bet the professors will load us up with the reading we missed."

"Do you think the other students are going to mob us and ask where we were?"

That got a full-on laugh. "Introvertians don't mob," Eza corrected gently. "However...I bet the topic will come up."

"The topic will come up," Cammie echoed in a singsong voice. "Like we haven't had the most interesting two weeks out of any student in the history of the Academy."

"The week you and I spent going to Exclaimovia has to be near the top of the list too."

"Ooooh, good point. So basically we have the top three most interesting weeks ever."

"That's the funny thing about us as dragon-companions, I guess. We live interesting lives so the rest of the kingdom doesn't have to. For most Introvertians, a quiet life of peace and family and good food is all we really want."

Cammie tilted her head at him. "Would you be happy with that?"

"I don't know. I really, really want to be a Ranger. I hear dad's stories, and Professor Grenalla's stories, and nothing gets me more excited." He glanced over at Cammie. "Your stories come pretty close, though."

"You're too kind," Cammie told him with a curtsy.

"But my dad gave all that up to spend more time with me, and he seems really happy now. Professor Grenalla gave it up to teach. And I know it would be really hard to have a family if I were a Ranger, because I'd be gone a lot." Eza stopped and thought for a moment. "I was going to say I'd give up all my dreams for love, but it wouldn't really be giving them up if I did it to gain a love people would write poems about."

"Stop right now. I have to write down that line." Cammie dropped her pack and fished around for some paper. "There's a one hundred percent chance it shows up in my next play."

"You're writing another one?"

"Not yet. But a true woman of the arts always has her eyes and ears open for ideas."

"And usually her mouth, too," Eza teased.

"You're lucky I'm writing at the moment or I'd be poking you so hard."

"Wait, does this mean I get co-writer credit for the play, since you're using my line?"

"Of course!"

"Excellent. I'm halfway to being stage-famous already."

Cammie giggled. "Not yet. I still have to write the rest of the play, and then we have to perform it. *Then* you can start bragging."

"An Introvertian bragging?" Eza asked, putting his hand on his chest with an air of surprised formality. "Such a thing has surely never happened, my lady."

"Hey, that's good acting."

"I have a good teacher."

Cammie was putting her papers back in her pack, but she looked up with a smile. "Thanks, Eza."

"Just being honest."

Cammie had been right, Eza realized: it felt *really good* to be sitting in History class and taking notes while Professor Ozara lectured about the origins of Telravia. The professor made it sound like everyone in Tranquility wanted to know all about their new ally – and most of them were *extremely* grossed out by what they learned. "Our information about Telravia is rather sparse," conceded Professor Ozara. "In past centuries, before we gave up magic, we had extensive contact with Telravia, so you would think the historians of the day would have written down what they had seen and learned. But that wasn't done. It's almost as if we preferred *not* to know about them, as if the information we'd learned was either too disgusting or too dangerous to be preserved. All we know for sure is that we used to fight them. I understand we have an ambassador with the Telravians now, so we'll see what he or she brings back to us. For now, here's what we know about the beginnings of the Telravian state."

"This should be good," Cammie whispered.

"This should be awful," Eza corrected.

"Most of you are at least somewhat aware of the fact that the five kingdoms are not all that exist. There is a sixth kingdom, Vagran, north of Claira, with which we have never had formal contact. There are scattered tribes north of Telravia, and probably quite a bit of civilization east of Esteria and southeast of Exclaimovia. The Exclaimovians, bordering the Great Sea as they do, have told stories of strange people they've met on their ocean travels, though it remains anyone's guess how much of that is true and how much is exaggeration."

"I'd go with ninety percent exaggeration," Cammie told Eza quietly.

"Only ninety?"

Professor Ozara continued. "The land that is now Telravia used to be inhabited by scattered tribes that seem to have discovered magic independently of each other at about the time Introvertia was being established. The strongest tribes quickly subjugated the weakest, but a curious thing happened. One would expect the strongest tribe to set up a system by which they would always be in control, but the Telrav tribe didn't do that. Rather, their system dictated that whichever tribe *became* the strongest would be in control. As Telravia grew, it moved away from a tribe-based system, but it kept the general principle that the strongest should rule. They're now governed by a council of seven sorcerers, and the only way to gain a seat on the council is to kill a counselor and take his or her position."

An audible murmur of disgust made its way around the class.

"Magical strength, in particular, is prized above all," Professor Ozara continued. "There are no limits, no rules, and no taboos on the pursuit of magical excellence. Telravia is very much a society in which *right* and *wrong* have no real meaning. *Right* is whatever brings strength, and *wrong* is whatever makes a person or a nation weak. As you might imagine, the darker forms of magic are prevalent in Telravia."

Lahan Meara, from Victory Company, raised his hand. "Professor, what do you mean by darker magic?"

Professor Ozara looked at the ceiling and then back to Lahan. "Do you have a strong stomach, Cadet?"

"I – think so, sir."

"Early Telravians were obsessed with the idea of bringing the dead back to life. Necromancy, they call it. You can never put the life-energy back into a body, once it's departed, but you can make the body itself stand up and move around. I believe their ultimate goal was to field an army of the dead, which could simply be raised again if they were 'killed' for a second time on the battlefield."

"I saw something like that," blurted Cammie. "Eza and I did. We saw a skeletal rotting dragon."

The murmur arose again, and someone said, "Skeletal dragon?"

"That kind of magic is supposed to be very difficult indeed," Professor Ozara said. "Bones cannot fly, so the spellcaster must be constantly expending magical energy in order to keep the creature in the air."

"That explains why they were mad when I killed it." Cammie thought about that. "Re-killed it."

Professor Ozara smiled thinly. "Unfortunately for Telravia but fortunately for the rest of us, necromancy does not appear to work the way they originally thought it did. It doesn't seem possible for one spellcaster to create and control an entire army of the dead. But the Telravians have also dabbled in mind control, attempting to place thoughts in someone's head or even get them to act against their own will. My personal belief is that we Introvertians would be largely immune to this, as we're typically quiet and in control of our own minds. Lastly...I hesitate to even talk about it, but Telravians have been quite successful at extending their own lives by draining the life-energy out of other creatures and into the spellcaster. This had most unfortunate consequences in the early days of the kingdom, when their sorcerers were not particular about *which* animals they drained life from, and what they found is that if you continually drain life from animals, you become more like an animal until you eventually stop being human at all."

Eza and Cammie gave nauseated grimaces to each other.

"I must restate that much of this is unconfirmed," the professor added. "There is really only one source for all this information about Telravia, and you know by now that we consider history to be basically certain when it is confirmed by three to four independent sources. But this is what we believe so far. Are there any questions?"

Lahan Meara's hand went up again. "Why exactly are we allied with these people, if they're so disgusting that the historians didn't even want to write anything down about them?"

"Cause of her," Razan said from across the room, pointing at Cammie. "Her people started a war against us because she's here."

In a flash Eza was up out of his seat, turning around to face Razan, but Cammie caught his hand. "He's not worth whatever you're about to do," she said quietly.

"That's right," Razan taunted, "hold your boyfriend back."

"Cadet Enara, you're out of line," Professor Ozara said. "You're dismissed from my class until further notice. That conduct is shameful for *any* Introvertian, and especially for a soldier in the king's army."

"Shameful is having *her* here," Razan said, not looking backward on his way out the door.

Eza sat back down, looking at Cammie to see her reaction, expecting to see fire in her eyes or on her hands. Instead she just shrugged. "I feel sorry for him," she told Eza.

He kept checking on Cammie through the rest of the lecture, but she truly seemed as if she'd brushed the whole thing off and was fully focused on the professor. Cammie was full of surprises, Eza thought. Sometimes little things set her off and sometimes she gracefully handled things he thought would make her explode.

"Want to have lunch with me?" he asked when the lecture was over.

"We have lunch every day," she said with a confused smile.

"I have a plan."

"Oh! Eza has a plan!" Cammie dramatically threw an arm across her forehead. "Lead on, fair prince!"

"So that thing with Razan bounces off you but you get dramatic about lunch?"

"I like to keep you guessing," Cammie reminded him.

They took a detour to the mess hall, where Eza picked up enough meat-filled pastry patties to satisfy both of them. "Okay," Cammie said, "now tell me where we're going."

"I like to keep you guessing," repeated Eza.

"You can't use my own line against me!"

"I can and I did. I know how you hate suspense and I'm going to torment you a little."

"I'll show you torment," Cammie declared, moving in to tickle Eza's sides.

But he quickly danced out of the way and turned to face Cammie. "Those are some nice meat pastries I have in my backpack," he said seriously. "It'd be a shame if something were to...*happen* to them." He pantomimed falling backward and squishing the pastries.

"You wouldn't," Cammie said, her eyes wide in

pretend horror.

"Tickle me again and find out," Eza said with a raised eyebrow.

"I'll take my chances." Cammie lunged toward Eza again, and he took off running out the mess hall and toward the stairs on the northeast corner.

He deliberately held back so Cammie could stay close, taking her up the stairs, down a short hall, around a corner, and up a long, tight spiral staircase. As they were nearing the top of the steps, he could hear her starting to breathe hard, but she didn't give up the chase. Eza crested the top step, hoping no one else just happened to be taking a picnic lunch in the northeast guard tower.

It wasn't really a guard tower anymore, now that there hadn't been an attack on Tranquility in centuries. During their first year at the Academy, Eza and Shanna had spent dozens of hours together up here, watching the horizon and pretending they were Rangers. He hadn't brought Cammie before, though, and her eyes widened when she huffed her way onto the platform and took in the sight. "It's...beautiful," she said softly.

In the clear spring afternoon they could see almost twenty miles. To the southeast the Impassable Mountains stabbed the cloudless sky, and to the northeast, flat plains stretched toward Claira. Cammie turned slowly in a circle and Eza followed her movement. They could see the trees and roofs of Tranquility sprawling off to the west and southwest, and Mazaren Fortress faintly visible over all the treetops. A gentle breeze pushed its way through the open sides of the tower, and Cammie breathed in. "This is wonderful, Eza. Thank you."

He offered her a meat patty. "Lunch?"

The stone walls and floor were cool beneath the wood roof, and once the food was gone, Cammie closed her eyes. "Now would be a great time for a nap. We have not gotten nearly enough rest over the past two weeks."

"Go right ahead." Eza slid his pack over for Cammie to use as a pillow, and she slid to the floor, her hands clasped over her belly button and her eyes already closed. On a whim he reached over and started massaging her scalp.

"Ooooh, that's worth putting off a nap for," she said, opening one eye.

So Eza kept playing with her hair, and eventually her eyes closed again. The satisfied smile on her face faded as her breathing got deeper and slower. She had time to sleep; Military Tactics class with Professor Rizara started at one o'clock, which wasn't for another hour, so Eza scratched her head for a while longer and then pulled out one of the books he'd gotten from Cappel's Bookstore the night before he and Cammie had first left for

Exclaimovia. That was only a month ago, but it seemed like forever. He could hardly even remember life before he'd had Cammie next to him, interrupting and shouting and doing all the other things he loved about her.

For some reason he couldn't concentrate on the book, so he put it back in his pack and closed his eyes, listening to the wind and to the sounds of the birds spiraling over the city – swallows, by the sound of them. This was as good as life got. A quiet spring afternoon, the sun hanging in a sky so blue it seemed endless, Cammie next to him. There was nothing better.

Eza and Cammie arrived back home late in the evening, nodding to the dozen guards posted all around the Skywing house. Denavi was standing barefoot in the garden, feeding Aleiza some pieces of raw meat and rubbing the dragon's neck. In response to Eza's look of confusion, Denavi smiled. "I hate shoes. I'd go the rest of my life without wearing them if I could."

"No, not that *at all,*" Eza said, trying not to laugh. "I'm surprised Aleiza let you get so close so quickly. She's not especially fond of new people. And she's *really* happy right now."

"Tell me how that works, the talking to dragons thing."

Eza had never really tried to put it into words before.

"It's like...in my head I can see what she's seeing, and she can see what I'm seeing. And we can pass thoughts to each other, not specific thoughts like the way you and I are talking to each other right now, but feelings. She can tell if I want her to come, if I want her to attack, or if I'm happy or sad. I can tell the same about her. I've only had her for about a month, but as we spend more time together, the thoughts we pass will become more precise. It'll eventually be a lot like talking, although maybe talking to a five- or six-year-old."

"That's so intriguing." Denavi scratched under Aleiza's chin. "Clairans have magical creatures, too, but we only use them for battle. They're trained to follow commands and that's all. The idea that you would be able to know how your dragon is feeling, and that you would care about it...we don't have anything like that."

"Is there a special meal you'd like for dinner?" Eza asked.

Denavi smiled. "Something Introvertian, perhaps? If this is going to be my new home, I should learn to eat like the locals."

"And something Exclaimovian, too," Cammie said excitedly. "Eza made me this blend of spices that tastes really good."

"What do you think, Aleiza?" Eza asked out loud. "Are you ready to grill some meat?"

Ezarra wasn't home yet by the time they all sat down to dinner, which was a little unusual but not worrisome. Eza left his father's plate in the outdoor oven so the hot stones would keep it warm until he arrived. The meal was chopped onala wraps, with meat grilled by Aleiza and finely sliced by Eza and then wrapped in fresh flatbread. Eza couldn't help but notice that Denavi finished her first and stealthily made a second; apparently she was still catching up from her days of not eating.

After the meal Denavi pushed her chair back from the table and stretched both arms up over her head. She was still borrowing one of Eza's shirts, which was just barely long enough for her, and the stretch made it lift several inches past her belly button. "What is *that*?" Eza blurted, pointing at an angry pockmarked scar on the left side of her stomach.

"Oh, that," Denavi said, quickly lowering her arms. "I got it in a fight against the Telravians."

"You were injured in battle?" Cammie clarified.

"Yes, I was. We won the fight, though." Denavi absent-mindedly reached under her shirt and fingered the scar. "It looked a lot worse before I used my healing magic on it."

"I want to know more about healing magic," Eza said.

"It's like any other kind of magic, I suppose, except

you can't attack with it. You can heal physical or magical wounds. I've heard that advanced spellcasters can even heal diseases. And the really elite ones can supposedly heal things that aren't even alive anymore, like repairing cracks in wooden buildings."

Eza leaned back. "That sounds fascinating. I wish I could do it."

"You can," Denavi said, confused. "You do Artomancy, right?"

"Yes..."

"There are quite a few Artomancers in Claira, and three of the people in my company were Artomancer-healers. I don't fully understand Artomancy myself, but as I understand it, there are certain things you can do, like growth and warmth."

"I can do both of those," Eza said excitedly.

"It had something to do with them. I'm sorry I can't give you the exact spells to cast. I wish I could be more useful." Denavi hung her head.

"It's okay," Cammie quickly assured her. "You told Eza something he didn't know. And he's pretty smart; I bet he can figure it out."

Wheels were already turning inside Eza's head. He'd made grass grow up from the ground in that fight against Denavi's company. If he could make new grass grow...couldn't he *regrow* something that had been injured, or cut, or torn? It couldn't possibly be that simple. He didn't know what muscle was *made* of, so how could he knit it together? Maybe Professor Norraza, his Artomancy instructor, would know, but Eza had only been to one Artomancy class before he'd been called away – and maybe Professor Norraza wouldn't know either...

"That's your concentration face," he heard Cammie saying, and the sound jolted him back to the present moment, where Cammie and Denavi were staring at him. "You're overthinking it," Cammie told him. "Look, my back hurts from sleeping on that stone floor. You can experiment on me if you want."

"I have no idea what I'm doing," Eza told her. "I could injure you."

"For you, I'll take the risk," she said, smiling gently at him.

Cammie stretched herself out on the couch, lying facedown. Eza got on his knees front of her, and Denavi went to stand behind Eza for a better view. With a deep breath, Eza laid his hands on Cammie's back and opened himself to the Artomancy magic. He thought of heat, and immediately Cammie appeared in front of him as a bright yellow light. A patch on the left side of her back was white, hotter than the rest. Maybe those were the sore muscles. Eza wiped the heat from his sight and thought of growth, but lightly, not wanting to accidentally make her sprout wings or something. Cammie tensed and immediately Eza stopped his magic. "What?" he asked fearfully.

"No, it felt good," Cammie said. "It was just...different. Do it again."

Eza looked back at Denavi, as if she would be able to tell him something, but she just tilted her head and looked at him with her dark eyes. This was all on Eza. He took another deep breath, terrified to hurt Cammie. At that moment she looked back at him, and he could see the trust in her eyes. If she trusted him, then he could trust himself. He reached out again with the growth and...

"Mmmmm," Cammie said. "That's *perfect*."

Eza switched to heat for a moment and saw the angry white parts had faded to yellow. "Do you feel better?" he asked her.

Cammie arched her back, then sat up and leaned forward. "All the pain is gone," she told him.

"Really?"

"Yeah," she said. "Now I can do this." She wrapped her arms around Eza in a hug, then picked him up and twirled him around before setting him down. "Ooooh, I think I just hurt my back again. I might need some more magic."

"Lie down, then."

Eza couldn't see any hot spots on her back this time, so he was pretty sure she'd just been teasing him, but he gently heated her lower back, then her ribs, then her shoulder blades, radiating warmth through the muscles. Cammie sagged in relaxation, as if she were being absorbed into the couch. "Whatever you're doing, don't ever stop," she told him.

He was going to protest that "ever" was a long time, but opted to keep his mouth shut. In less than five minutes, Cammie was asleep, her breathing so deep and slow that it was almost like she was snoring. Eza sat back, wondering whether to wake her up and send her upstairs to her bed or just let her stay on the couch. In the end he opted for something he'd often done while they were traveling to Exclaimovia; he bounced up the stairs, brought her blankets down, and covered her. There was still light streaming in through the windows, so Eza dug out the book he'd tried to start earlier in the guard tower and sat down next to Cammie's head, listening to the soft sound of her breathing.

FIFTEEN

Denavi could not *believe* how oblivious Eza was. Even a blind carraga goat could see that he loved Cammie, and that she loved him too. Did he really think, when she said "for you, I'll take the risk," that she was only talking about the pain in her back? *Zero* chance, thought Denavi. Cammie was sending him a message loud and clear, but *whoosh*, it had flown right over his head. The kid might be able to tell eighty different kinds of animals from their droppings, but he was missing the most obvious signs in the world.

Maybe it wasn't entirely his fault. Eza had told her a bit about Introvertia when they were marching back to Tranquility, before he'd given up and let Cammie do all the talking. Denavi was fairly sure she remembered him saying that Introvertians were honest and direct, that they didn't say one thing and mean another – which was the opposite of what Denavi had always been told about them. Perhaps he was simply used to people speaking their minds. If Cammie wanted him to know she wanted him to court her, she'd either have to come right out and say it, or she'd have to send an *extremely* unsubtle message.

Still, Denavi wanted to scream it at him. There he

was, sitting by Cammie while she slept, protecting her with his presence. He *had* to know he was deeply in love with her. His father had said that Eza would have to figure it out in his own time, but what was he waiting for? Denavi knew it wasn't her place to ask, not yet. She kept her mouth shut, but couldn't keep from shaking her head slightly in amazement.

Ezarra came in the front door then, and Eza quietly stood, careful not to disturb Cammie, before running to his father. The two shared a hug so long and so warm it made the corner of Denavi's mouth tug down. She hadn't hugged her own father in – had it really been nine years? Everyone had said he'd brought honor to the family, had lived and died as the Noble Enlightened Warrior, but the war hadn't changed anything; Vagran and Claira still had the same borders they'd had before, still had the same governments and philosophies. The only thing that changed was the thousands of families destroyed by dead and wounded dads and wives and sons and sisters. If Claira thought that "honor" meant "dying a meaningless death without complaint," then Denavi was more grateful than ever to be out of the place.

Eza had taken his seat by Cammie's head again. Ezarra was walking past Denavi's couch on his way to the kitchen, and paused just as he was passing her. "Are you alright?" he asked.

Denavi cleared her throat, keeping her head down.

"You're not alright," he said softly.

Denavi looked up at him, trying to keep from getting soggy-eyed. Eza had talked about growing up without a mother, which meant that Ezarra was someone who'd known pain and loss. He would understand what she was feeling. "No," she confessed. See, Ezarra could pick up on small things! Why couldn't Eza?

Ezarra held out his arms, and without any hesitation Denavi rose and let herself be wrapped up in them. So this was what a father's hug felt like. She didn't even know she'd been crying until she finally pulled away and saw Ezarra's shirt soaked where her head had been pressed against him. "I'm sorry," Denavi said, wiping her eyes. "My dad died in battle a long time ago."

"I know I'm not your father," Ezarra said. "I never will be. Nothing can fill that hole. But as long as you're here, I can treat you like one of my kids if you want me to."

Denavi nodded mutely, unable to even voice her gratitude, but Ezarra welcomed her when she moved in for another long hug. If anyone in Claira had seen her crying in the arms of someone she barely knew, she'd have been laughed out of the place. The longer she was here in Introvertia, the more glad she was about leaving Claira.

Ezarra ate his dinner and went upstairs, leaving Denavi and Eza alone with the sleeping Cammie. Denavi knew it wasn't any of her business to say anything to Eza, knew she risked upsetting him if she got involved, but she decided to go for it. Aleiza and Neemie thumped their snouts against the back door, and Eza got up to let them in. Neemie curled up next to Eza while Aleiza sprawled out on the floor and dropped her head into Eza's lap.

"Can I talk to you, Eza?" Denavi asked.

"I think you already are," he said with a small smile. "But sure. Go right ahead."

Denavi pushed her hair back behind her ears so Eza could see the earnestness on her face. "At the Military Institute, we learned a lot about the way people think. We learned how to analyze our enemies, to look for weaknesses that we could use against them. Can I tell you something I've noticed about you?"

"Oh, this should be fun," he said, his smile widening.

"I notice you're wearing your boots inside the house. Everyone else takes them off at the door, probably to keep the dirt out, but you wear them all the time. Bare feet mean vulnerability, because you can't easily run away from a situation or fight your way out of it. You value always being prepared. Your battle plans are probably safe, cautious. Maybe too cautious. You don't like taking risks."

"You got all that from the fact that I'm wearing boots?"

"Tell me I'm wrong, then."

Eza sat back, looking Denavi in the eyes. "No, you're right. I hate being barefoot, for exactly the reasons you described. I don't ever want to be caught unprepared."

This was where Denavi had to tread lightly. "So...if you're the kind of person who is afraid of taking risks, who maybe plays it a little *too* safe...do you think there might be any other areas in your life where you're doing that? Where there's a risk you ought to be taking but you're letting fear hold you back?"

Eza stared at her for so long that Denavi thought he might have fallen asleep with his eyes open. "I guess you must trust us a lot, then," he said at last, pointing at her feet. "I haven't seen you with shoes on since you got here."

Cammie had said that Exclaimovians often changed the topic when they didn't like where a conversation was going. Eza must have picked that up from her; it seemed out of character for an Introvertian to do anything other than answer a direct question. But Denavi sensed that now wasn't the time to press the topic; she had given him something to think about, so now she ought to let him think.

"I like it here," Denavi said. "You've all been nothing but friendly to me, and I appreciate that. And yes, I do feel...at ease, I suppose, in a way that I really never did back home. I don't want to be a fighter, and I never did, but that life was forced on me from childhood. The idea of the Noble Enlightened Warrior is idolized by my people, and everyone is forced into that mold, whether they fit it or not." She snorted a one-note laugh. "I guess they figured the best way to pay me back for my dad dying in battle was giving me the chance to die in battle, too."

"In Introvertia you can be anything you want to be," Eza said. "You can start your whole life over. What do you want to do?"

"I don't know," Denavi admitted. "I don't know what I *can* do. All I know is war. I mean, I've memorized an awful lot of Clairan poetry, but I don't guess people would pay money for that here."

"You'd be surprised. Introvertians are pretty open-minded, for the most part. Besides, you have healing magic. I bet you could get paid to use that, or to teach it to other people."

Denavi considered that. "I could. But that doesn't really...feel like *it,* if you know what I mean. It doesn't feel like *the thing* I want to spend the rest of my life doing."

"How old are you, anyway? Eighteen?"

"Seventeen. In Clairan society I wouldn't be an adult until I'd completed three more years of military service."

"Introvertians become adults at thirteen. You're a grown-up here."

"So you and Cammie could get married if you wanted to."

Denavi hadn't meant to say it, but the words were out there, hanging in midair. Her fingers tightened on the sofa cushions; she was expecting Eza to get mad at her and chide her for overstepping her boundaries. Instead that soft smile, which had hardly left his face the whole time they'd talked, stayed where it was. "Not just yet," Eza said. There was no anger in his green eyes. "Our Age of First Marriage is seventeen, so we couldn't do that just yet. But we could court until we were old enough."

Denavi cleared her throat and looked at the floor. "It's, um, late. I should probably get to bed." *Before I accidentally run my mouth again*, she added silently.

"Thank you for talking with me," Eza said, and Denavi felt like he really meant it.

That had gone pretty well, Denavi thought to herself as she tiptoed up the stairs and quietly opened the door to her bedroom. Moonlight was trickling through the window in her bedroom, lighting up her path to the bed as she climbed underneath the soft blankets. That conversation with Eza had been...*fun*. It had felt like a mental duel, where Denavi was feinting and thrusting and Eza was trying to parry. But Denavi was sure her final blows had landed. Actually, she was dying to know whether he'd fall asleep thinking about what she said.

Probably not, she decided. He'd most likely fall asleep thinking of Cammie.

A soft but solid thudding startled Cammie the next morning. She woke up slowly, as if rising to the surface of the ocean after being a hundred feet down, and by the time she opened her eyes, the thudding had sounded for a second time. She had no idea where she was, but she felt Eza rise next to her – somehow, even with her eyes closed, she could tell it was him – and open the door. That was it. Someone was knocking on a door.

At last Cammie forced her eyes open and sat up. The last thing she remembered from the night before was some kind of magical massage from Eza, which was officially one of the best experiences of her life. Eza was talking to someone at the front door, and then the someone was coming inside. Cammie stood up and turned around to see what was happening.

It was one of the king's messengers, the same one who had tracked her and Eza down in the mess hall so long ago when the Exclaimovian delegation had demanded Cammie's return. Cammie shuddered at the thought. Words could not describe her gratitude to King Jazan and Queen Annaya for keeping her safe.

"The Clairans and Esterians are on the move," the messenger was saying. "Our scouts have reported a combined force marching out from Arkiana directly toward the city of Resolve, fifty miles north of here. We're told that our Telravian allies are already on the way to meet us. You and Cadet Ravenwood are to report to Mazaren Fortress with all possible speed. Your Clairan guest must, to the king's great regret, remain here at your home until you return."

"At the king's service," Eza responded, and then the messenger was gone.

"There's going to be a battle?" Cammie asked, still not fully awake. Aleiza was on the ground near the sofa; she had probably spent the night with her head on Eza's stomach, the way she liked to do. Aleiza let out an adorable dragon-yawn, then blinked a few times at Eza and put her silver-gray head back on the ground.

"It sounds like it. Maybe the Clairans and Esterians will retreat once they see us allied with Telravia."

Cammie was quiet for several moments. "I wonder where my people are."

"It is very strange that he didn't mention Exclaimovia, isn't it?"

"But they're the ones who started this war in the first place. Why wouldn't they be there? Do you think they're going to attack through the Very Large Forest while our army is preoccupied?"

"I'm sure the king and his generals have thought of that," Eza reassured her. "We don't have to worry about it. We have our orders."

"Maybe you Silent Ones can turn off your minds," Cammie groused. "The rest of us can't."

"I bet I can turn off your mind." The next thing Cammie knew, Eza was standing behind her, his fingers gently massaging her scalp right behind her ears.

"Oooooh...yep, that did it. I don't care about anything at all right now." Cammie closed her eyes.

Eza rubbed her head for several minutes, then rested his hands on her shoulders. "The messenger did say *with all possible speed*. We'd better get going."

"How does my hair look?"

"You have an incredible case of bed head. I guess it's actually couch head. But you still look absolutely beautiful."

Cammie put her hands on her cheeks to try and hide her blushing.

Eza was smiling at her reaction. "Now get dressed. We have to go."

"Are you going to tell Denavi where we're going?"

"I am. It wouldn't be right not to." He turned around to head for the staircase.

"Do you think she'll be upset that she doesn't get to come with us?" Cammie asked.

"She told me last night that she didn't want to be a warrior. She might be lonely here by herself, but I don't think she'll be disappointed about missing a battle against her old home. There might be people she knows on the other side and that would be hard."

"Hm. I didn't think about that."

Cammie followed Eza up the stairs and stood next to him as he tapped on Denavi's bedroom door. Denavi opened the door a few moments later, one eye closed and her dark hair poofing out from her head in every direction. "Good morning," Eza told her. "Cammie and I have been ordered out. There's going to be a big battle, and you have to stay here."

"Okay," Denavi said."Be safe, please."

"We'll do our best," Eza promised. "We have to take Aleiza with us because she's my companion, but Neemie will stay. She can help you cook dinner and heat up bath water. Any of the books in the downstairs bookcase are yours to read." He hesitated. "Do you want me to see if my friend Shanna can come over and spend some time with you while we're gone? I don't know if she's deploying too, but I don't think they'd be sending all the

Academy students."

Denavi smiled. "If she's a friend of yours, then I'd love to meet her."

"I'll send her a message before we leave. I hope we come back soon."

"Me too."

Cammie put her hand on Eza's back. "That was really smart, to introduce her to Shanna. You're really thoughtful."

She realized what she'd done at the same moment Eza smiled widely. "Cammaina Ravenwood, did you just compliment me?"

Cammie covered her mouth, then frantically began wiping her sleeve on Eza's shoulder. "RUB! BACK! OFF!"

"That's the second time you've complimented me lately," Eza told her as he headed into his bedroom to pack his clothes and gear.

"Is not. When was the first?"

"When we were dancing. You said I was a good leader, and I called you by your full name and asked if you'd just complimented me."

"Your memory is really good." Cammie's was better; she had perfect recall and never forgot anything, but she chose not to remind Eza of that. It wasn't that she'd forgotten she'd complimented him during the dance;

she'd just been stating a fact, so she didn't think of it as a compliment.

Maybe that was the trick to giving and receiving them without panicking, she thought – to think of them as normal rather than unusual. She'd have to practice that.

"Well," he said, turning a little red, "I had a lot of fun dancing with you, and I hope I remember that forever."

"Ezalen Skywing, are you blushing?"

"Please. Don't pretend you didn't do the same thing earlier when I said you looked beautiful."

Cammie clenched her jaw, hoping to hide her smile. "You weren't supposed to see that."

"I can do it again if you want. You look really beautiful this morning."

Cammie tried her hardest to keep a straight face as she looked into his green eyes, and after about five seconds she failed. A goofy smile cracked her face and she looked down. *It's normal for him to say things like that,* she reminded herself. "Thank you, Eza."

He hoisted his pack onto his shoulder. "Is there anything you want me to carry for you?"

"Well, you know, I have my fourteen changes of clothes, twelve hair ribbons, perhaps a portable stage in case we want to perform a play while we're out..."

"I love your sense of humor."

Cammie gave a curtsy. "It's what I do."

Eza disappeared back into his room and came out with a pouch of something. Cammie craned her neck to get a look at it. "What's that?"

"You'll see."

"ARRRRRGGHHHHH," she bellowed. "I DON'T LIKE SUSPENSE."

That just amused Eza even more, so Cammie pretended to sulk as she followed him down the stairs and to the kitchen table, where he scribbled a letter to Shanna and sent it off with Neemie. It was Saturday morning, so Shanna would probably not be at Carnazon, but Eza must have known where her house was, so that he could give Neemie a mental picture. While his back was turned, she snuck a peek into the pouch.

"Why are you leaving money here?"

"Denavi seems to like wearing Introvertian clothes, so maybe Shanna can go buy some for her."

"That's incredibly kind."

Eza shrugged. "The look on her face will bring me way more satisfaction than whatever I would have bought for myself."

Aleiza was waiting for them by the front door and took wing as soon as Eza and Cammie stepped outside. Cammie had to admit that Tranquility's weather was nearly perfect. Exclaimovia often got strong storms blowing off the Great Sea, but Introvertia wasn't directly on the sea, and something about the proximity of the mountains must have blown storms off track before they arrived. She had to work hard to remember the last time she'd seen a cloud in the sky over Tranquility.

A shadow weaved back and forth across the road as Aleiza banked left and right over their heads. "You know," Cammie admitted, "I feel like I'm getting just a little bit more used to Tranquility. I mean the slower pace and the, ah, lower volume. It's not...*relaxing,* exactly, but it doesn't feel ominous and creepy the way it did at first."

"That's good," Eza told her.

"I do have to say I understand how the Clairans had the wrong idea about Introvertia, though. You've been surrounded by this your whole life, and I don't think you fully understand how *unusual* it is to live in a place where silence is normal and people just say what they mean without playing mind games with each other."

"Why would anyone want to do it differently? Who likes mind games?"

"Oh, nobody." Cammie reached up and absently started to braid the side of her hair as they walked. "But...in most places, you can't be honest with just anybody. You never know who they might blab it to, or whether they might keep it away somewhere to use against you later."

"That sounds horrible."

"Don't get me wrong. The more I'm here, the more I love it. I adore not having to second-guess every word that comes out of my mouth, wondering who might take it the wrong way, because I know Introvertians don't think like that." She took a deep breath, not sure how to end her thought. "I'm just saying that your people have something really special, and I can totally understand why people who aren't you might think there's no way it could be real."

"So you love Introvertia because you don't have to think before you speak," repeated Eza.

Cammie exploded into laughter. "Well, if you put it that way..."

"I'm just teasing."

"But you're on to something. People shouldn't have to hide their true selves *anywhere.* We should all be surrounded by people who love and accept us as we are, and speak their true thoughts to us without trying to hide things or manipulate us. If the whole world could be like Introvertia, I bet there'd be a lot less anger and a lot less war. I mean, I could go up to that lady over there and tell her I was having a great day, and she'd probably ask me why and listen for fifteen minutes while I told her. That's not *normal,* Eza. You can't really blame places like Exclaimovia and Claira for not being able to understand you."

"I don't really care whether strangers understand me or not. I just want them to leave us alone so we can live in peace the way we want."

Cammie took Eza's hand, wrapping her fingers around his. "Relax. You're tense."

"Was it that obvious?"

"No, it wasn't obvious. I just know you really well."

She could see his shoulders drop as he took a big breath. "Thanks."

"You'd do the same for me."

Nothing could have prepared Cammie for the sight that greeted her at Mazaren Fortress – or rather, outside it. She couldn't even get inside because of the mass of soldiers clogging the streets outside, blue and silver armor and banners from sidewalk to sidewalk. Eza led her out the nearby gate and to the plain just north of Tranquility, where infantry and cavalry stretched out almost as far as the eye could see and *thousands* of dragons spiraled gracefully overhead. Aleiza flew off to join them, a full two feet taller than the largest one out there, belching flame into the crisp spring air.

"How many troops do you think are here?" she asked Eza quietly.

"The standing army is forty thousand strong," he answered, leading her over toward the quartermaster to pick up their own uniforms and light armor. "And this looks like juuuuust about all of them."

"Denavi said Esteria's army was seventy thousand and Claira's was almost a hundred thousand." Cammie realized she was squeezing Eza's hand really tightly, but he hadn't complained. "We're going to be outnumbered."

"Telravia will help." Eza helped Cammie put on her lightweight metal breastplate, smoothing out the thigh guards and making sure her long-sleeved undershirt hadn't bunched up. The infantry wore thicker armor that covered more of their bodies, but archers – and now spellcasters – were decked out for mobility instead.

"Yay," Cammie said flatly. "Great. The grossest people in the known world are going to help us."

"There's Colonel Ennazar!" Eza said, pointing. "I wonder if he's going to come. It would be great to have him with us."

The colonel spotted Eza looking at him and a smile broke out on his face. In seconds he was standing face to face with Cammie and Eza. "Cadets. It's good to see you here."

"Yes, sir!" said Eza.

"I never got a chance to thank you for the work you did on your last mission. The information you gathered about the magical nodes was extremely helpful. Several of the units you see in front of you spent the last week training at the triple node you found."

"What happened to the huge dragon there?" Cammie asked.

"It flew away, much to our disappointment. We were hoping to study it, or perhaps befriend it. There's no telling where it might have ended up. Regardless, we'll be deploying elemental magic on the battlefield for the first time in eight hundred years, thanks to you two. I can't say enough what an incredible job you've done." He took a breath. "And bringing back that Clairan captive? Cadet Skywing – may I call you Ezalen? – you have no idea at all, *no idea* at all, how useful her information has been to us. She told us everything, from the size of the Clairan army to its composition to its battle tactics. If we win this battle – when we win this battle – I will personally thank her."

He really was babbling, Cammie thought.

"Yes, sir," Eza said again. "What are our orders in this battle?"

"You won't be on the front lines. The Telravians seem to think that you're some sort of magical ambassadors to them, since you came with Ambassador Gezana to that first meeting, so they're expecting your presence. Other than that..." Colonel Ennazar held out his hands. "Stay alive, and don't upset the Telravians."

He set off again without saying goodbye, and a few minutes later the horns were blowing for the soldiers to march. It took a long time for the whole army to get moving, Cammie thought, and she and Eza fell in with the rest of the dragon-companions. Cammie had wondered if perhaps there would be marching songs or people chanting cadences, but it was silent – not the relaxing silence of Tranquility, but the ominous silence she'd mentioned to Eza.

And why shouldn't it be silent? These people hadn't fought a war in centuries, and now they had no choice. They were vastly outnumbered, and allied with the most horrifying army Cammie could have imagined, with everything on the line. If they lost...

SIXTEEN

Eza had been in danger before. When Azanna had attacked Cammie and him on the way to Exclaimovia, he hadn't been scared – but it had happened so quickly that he hadn't had time to feel *anything*, only to react. When he and Cammie had gone into Pride, he still hadn't been scared – but he was disguised as an Exclaimovian, and as long as his cover wasn't blown, there was nothing to worry about. Of course, it had been blown, but even when he was captured he hadn't been scared – he was just in survival mode at that point, thinking about what he needed to do in order to get out of the situation.

So he shouldn't have been scared at the moment, he tried to convince himself, yet there was the fear, lurking in his stomach and making it hard to breathe. Maybe this was different. After all, this time he knew what was going to happen and there was no way around it. At the end of this three-day march, there would be a giant battle. This wasn't Eza being suddenly attacked by Azanna and responding on instinct. This was a slow walk toward a battle that might end not just in defeat for Introvertia, but death for Eza or even the end of Introvertia as a kingdom. It was impossible not to be scared.

But Eza appeared to be the only one who felt that way. The soldiers around him seemed confident, professional. If they were nervous at all, it didn't show. This was what they'd been trained to do, and when it was time to act, they'd do their very best.

And for some reason, the one person who could have made Eza feel better had suddenly decided that she was going to become a model Introvertian, lost in her own world and allergic to conversation. Cammie had brought a thick notebook with her and had spent almost every waking moment scribbling in it. Eza knew she probably wouldn't have minded if he'd interrupted her, and would probably have appreciated him talking about his fears with her. Still, she looked so deep in thought that Eza couldn't bring himself to drag her attention away from the page.

At evening on the third day, the Introvertian army came to a halt in the middle of a plain. Seven or eight miles off to the northeast, Eza could see thick woods. "That's probably where the Clairans and Esterians are waiting for us," he told Cammie. "Since we use dragons, we like to fight on open terrain, where the dragons can fly and maneuver freely. We don't like to fight where there are trees or other obstacles. The Clairans want us to come to them."

"Are we going to?"

"No, for two reasons. First, we're outnumbered. If you're outnumbered, you almost never attack, unless you have something really devious planned."

"Introvertians don't *do* devious, I've noticed."

Eza allowed himself a smile. "In battle, maybe sometimes. The second reason is that we're the defenders. Claira and Esteria are attacking us. If they want to get to Introvertia, they have to get through us, which means we pick the terrain and they have to come at us on our terms."

"What if they don't?"

"Then we go for the stomach. If we stay here for a few days and nobody moves, we'll send our dragons to harass their supply convoys and destroy their food wagons. It's hard to fight on an empty stomach. They'll have to attack or go back home."

Cammie adjusted her glasses, her one blue eye and one brown eye examining the empty plain in front of them. "Where are the Telravians?"

But there was an eerie green glow to the northwest, off toward Telravia, and as the night grew darker the glow seemed even brighter. Then over a slight rise came the front line of Telravian soldiers, their armor shining an otherworldly color. They chanted as they marched, and the song was not in any language Eza had ever heard. The hair on the back of his neck stood up and the other soldiers around him immediately grabbed their weapons. In the sky above them a cloud rose, a hideous green cloud that formed the shape of a laughing skull before wisping away into the night air.

Utter silence fell over the Introvertian camp.

"Well," Eza said at last, "I hope they scare the Clairans half as much as they just scared me."

Cammie wrapped her arms around him as if he were the only thing that could keep her safe from the Telravians.

In fact, she didn't let go of him. The soldiers camped in battle array, with the infantry on the front lines, the archers and the few companies of elemental sorcerers behind them, and the dragon-companions at the rear. Aleiza fell asleep to Eza's right with her snout on his stomach, but Cammie set up her sleeping back right next to Eza's. Very carefully, trying not to upset the already dozing Aleiza, Eza reached over and started rubbing Cammie's head.

He didn't know exactly when he'd fallen asleep, but he awoke just before dawn. Cammie was still lying next to him, but her arm was draped across his shoulders. Aleiza was snoring lightly as usual, her right wing covering his legs and her left up near his head. Eza was stuck. With no better idea, he tried mind-linking with Aleiza, wondering if perhaps he could see what she was dreaming about.

It didn't work and Aleiza awoke with a start, staring at Eza in confusion. "Sorry," he whispered to her. "I have an idea, though. Do you think you can scout the field?"

There was a risk, Eza knew, and he knew Aleiza had to have known it too. But the pre-dawn was still so dark that a single dragon would be very hard to see, and her massive size meant that any archer or spellcaster who wanted to take a shot at her would almost certainly assume she was smaller and further away than she really was. Aleiza whooshed gracefully into the air, and Eza linked minds with her, watching through her eyes.

Even in the dark Aleiza could pick up deep red Clairan banners all throughout the forest, and brilliant purple Esterian flags behind them. Eza tried to count the banners, hoping that the information would be useful to Colonel Ennazar or one of the other leaders, but Aleiza was moving too quickly and all he got was a best guess of seventy-four. He didn't know what that meant, but maybe Colonel Ennazar would.

At dawn, blood-chilling screams came from the Telravian camp, and any Introvertian soldiers who weren't already awake sprang up with their scanas in hand. The wailing and howling continued for half an hour, and by the end Eza was ready to surrender just to make it stop. Was that their battle cry, designed to terrify the enemy? Or were they – Eza recalled with horror what Professor Ozara had told them – draining the life-force from innocent people to make their army stronger before the battle?

Eza could see General Nazoa on horseback, riding from one side of the front line to the other, urging the soldiers to prepare for battle. He was just in time. From the trees on the right side of the Introvertian line, a furious mob of Esterians beneath their purple banners came charging. The fight had begun.

The front line of Esterian soldiers stood no chance. Advancing over open terrain, without any aerial cover, they were obliterated by fire from seven thousand screeching Introvertian dragons. Aleiza had led the assault, swooping low over the soldiers and spewing a long trail of flame that scorched flesh and baked armor. But no sooner had the first line fallen than another followed behind them, this one with huge scorpions at the front. The dragons banked again, diving in formation, and even from a hundred yards away Eza could hear the cracking and splintering of arachnid shells from dragon fire. A few of the scorpions skittered closer and closer to the Introvertian front lines; at last a final desperate strafing run from the dragons torched the bugs just twenty yards short of the Introvertian infantry.

But Esterian arrows were slicing through the air now, along with the occasional purple lance of primal magic. Aleiza instantly led the dragons to a higher altitude where the arrows couldn't reach, although magical energy still could, and there the dragons circled. For several minutes the battlefield was silent except for the distant flapping of dragon wings and sporadic magical potshots from the Esterians. Even the Telravians were quiet.

"What are they all waiting for?" Cammie asked Eza.

"Denavi told us that the Esterians often ran fake attacks to clear the way for Claira to charge with overwhelming force. I wouldn't be surprised if they made another strong feint on our right flank, in the hopes that we'd shift our formation, and then drive hard at the weak spot in our lines when we move to the right."

The Esterian battle cry sounded again, and this time thousands and thousands of troops, maybe thirty thousand of them, poured out of the woods directly toward the Introvertian right flank. Scorpions swarmed among them, and many of the Esterians rode enormous dogs, wolves maybe, that reached up to Eza's shoulders. Next to those the Introvertian dragons looked like children's toys. General Nazoa was only thirty yards from Eza now, still atop his horse, and Eza could see him debating whether to shift the formation. Colonel Ennazar had said all the leaders had been briefed on the tactics Denavi had told them during her interrogation...

But what if she really was a spy? The thought crashed through Eza's head and wouldn't leave. It didn't seem possible; she'd been so friendly with him, and cried in his father's arms. If she was faking all of that, she was an actress so good she'd make Cammie quit in frustration. Besides, the Introvertian generals wouldn't commit their entire army to a battle plan they hadn't triple-checked ahead of time...right?

Again the dragons roared out of the sky, but this time the Esterians were ready. A hail of arrows and a thousand beams of primal energy surged up to meet them. Eza watched in horror as dozens of dragons pinwheeled out of the sky, flopping to the ground, where they were finished off by jeering Esterian soldiers. Aleiza led this charge like she'd led all the others, drawing most of the Esterian fire, but she banked and dodged and swooped before laying waste to a long column of archers and spellcasters. Behind her a thousand more dragons blasted fire, and a thousand more behind them. But the magic and the arrows were taking their toll, and nearly a hundred dragons fell in that assault.

The Esterians were still getting the worst of it. The charge seemed to falter, and at that moment the Introvertian elemental mages opened up. A furious rain of fireballs and lightning bolts hurtled across the no-man's-land between the two armies, slicing down hundreds of warriors and scorpions and wolves. Eza could tell the magic was nowhere near as strong as what Cammie could do – but something was better than nothing. The Esterians fired back with primal magic, and angry purple lances made dirt explode into the sky in front of and behind the Introvertian lines, and occasionally in between them. Eza pulled Cammie down with him onto the ground, trying to make them smaller targets. *I could heal the wounded,* he told himself as a massive lance pounded the middle of the battle line and sent Introvertian soldiers sailing in all directions. But he wasn't allowed to, was under orders to stay alive. He couldn't go running to the front line...

And then a different battle shout sounded from off to Eza's left – the Clairans were sprinting out of the woods, streaming toward the split between the Introvertian and Telravian lines. The Introvertian dragons and sorcerers were already occupied with the Esterians and could do nothing about this new threat. The Telravians could – but they sat unmoving. What were they waiting for? Their armor was no longer glowing green the way it had the night before; maybe that spell had been an illusion or the magic had worn off. What a strange thing to notice with a battle raging around him, Eza thought. Perhaps his mind was just desperately searching around for something normal to think about, instead of the chaos and the death and the screams –

When the Clairans were two-thirds of the way to the Introvertian line, screeching echoed out of the forest, and tens of thousands of birds – combat falcons, Denavi had said – surged into the sky. That was apparently what the Telravians had been waiting for. Fifty thousand bolts of primal energy shattered the air, answered by fire and lightning and ice from the Clairan elemental mages. Immediately the Clairan charge shifted course, heading directly for the Telravians, as the roar of fireballs and thunder from the lightning mixed with excited shouts of charging soldiers and agonized howls from the wounded. It was like nothing Eza had ever heard before and he never wanted to hear it again.

Esteria had reached the Introvertian front now, and the Introvertian infantry leaped into action, scanas glinting in the faint morning sunlight. Even in the ugliness of battle Eza couldn't help admire the courage of the troops as they fought shoulder to shoulder, for each other and for their homeland. Archers behind the front line fired over the heads of the infantry in front of them, thinning out the Esterian lines and sending wolves and men tumbling to the dirt.

Eza opened his mind link to Aleiza, who had led the

dragons up to a higher altitude again, watching for the right opportunity to dive and attack. They could have done a lot of damage with an attack on the rear of the Clairans as they sprinted toward the Telravians, but the Clairan army was well organized and dangerous, and Eza had a bad feeling about what would happen when the dragons got over their heads. But he had a sudden idea. He tried feeding magical energy to Aleiza through the mind link, as if he were casting a spell – not any particular spell, just unformed magic.

The power surged through Aleiza, who immediately roared in satisfaction and took off on a solo assault toward the Esterian rear. With all the soldiers facing the other direction, they noticed too late as Aleiza descended on them and cut loose with a stream of fire more intense than any she'd ever unleashed before. It was as if Eza's energy were pouring back out of her. She banked up again, but through his own eyes Eza saw something – one of the Esterians sent a strong primal lance in her direction – it was heading straight for her –

Eza cast a rainbow door *through the mind link* and watched through his own eyes as one side of it opened below Aleiza and the other side directly above her. The lance passed right though both doors, completely missing Aleiza in the middle. He could tell his dragon had no idea what had just happened; he'd never felt such incredible confusion from her. All he could do was try to reassure her that he was protecting her, and feed her more magical energy as seven thousand dragons rallied around her for an assault on the Esterian front lines...

Not a moment too soon, either, because the Introvertian infantry were wavering until the exact moment the dragons blasted down into the Esterian rear. Eza could hear wails from the dying Esterians, and then the dragons were surging over his head, with scattered arrows and primal lances following them through the air as they cast a huge, rippling shadow over the Introvertian lines. The Esterians broke off and began to pull back, chased for just a few moments by the Introvertians until an order from General Nazoa broke off the pursuit. Introvertia was still outnumbered, after all, and overextending their lines would be suicide. The elemental spellcasters harassed the retreating Esterians with more fire and lightning, dodging bursts of primal magic in return. In fifteen minutes the Esterians had melted back into the forest.

To Eza's left, the Clairans were pulling back, too. It looked like they'd done significant damage to the Telravians, although they'd left an awful lot of casualties behind when they withdrew. Now that the immediate threat was over, Eza knew he had to do something. His healing magic was about to get its first real test.

Cammie grabbed his shirt even before he'd finished standing up. "Where are you going?"

"To heal some people."

She said nothing, but Eza could see the fear in her eyes as she clung to his shirt.

"I'll be careful," he promised.

"I'd be happier if you could be invisible." Cammie's eyes got wide. "Eza, what's going on in your head? You got that faraway-thinking look you sometimes get."

"Invisible..."

It should be simple, shouldn't it? One of the first Artomancy spells he'd ever cast was to change the colors of his clothes so he could sneak into Exclaimovia. That was just a trick of the light, Gar had told him. How much harder would it really be to change it so that light...wrapped around him?

Eza closed his eyes and reached out with all his senses, feeling the pale sunlight on his face, the short grass beneath his boots and the stony soil beneath that. A cool wind blew from the northwest, from Telravia, brushing Eza just behind his left ear as he stared at the battlefield. He spun the magic around himself like a caterpillar weaving a cocoon and –

Cammie gasped. "Where'd you go?"

"Right here."

"No way," she said in wonder, reaching out and

wrapping her hand around his ankle. "How did you do that?"

"Artomancy. Same way I turned my shirt purple."

Cammie giggled. "That doesn't seem like the same thing at all, but okay."

One thing Eza hadn't expected was that staying invisible seemed to drain his energy slowly. When he'd changed the color of his shirt, that was a single spell, but it was as if this spell had to be fed new power moment by moment. He'd have to hurry.

He sprinted toward the front lines, sliding to a halt next to the first wounded Introvertian he could find, who had a sword slice from her knee to her thigh. There was no time to hesitate like he had with Cammie. Eza reached out with *growth*, squeezing his eyes tight and imagining the soldier's skin knitting itself back together. Her groans of pain immediately subsided, and she lay back, exhausted but healed.

Eza spent the next hour healing as many Introvertians as he could find, and had to explain at least a hundred times why nobody could see him. It would have been a lot easier to just be visible, he thought – it would make the healing simpler if he wasn't splitting his focus between two different kinds of spells – but Colonel Ennazar's orders had been to stay alive, and he couldn't risk someone on the other side recognizing him – or even just taking a shot at the battlefield healer.

It was lunchtime by then, and even though Eza didn't want to eat, he knew it was important to keep his strength up. A lot of the other soldiers probably felt the same way – and even more so, since they'd been in the thick of the combat. Eza had watched the carnage from a distance, but he couldn't imagine what it would be like to see a friend or comrade slashed apart next to him, how it would feel to see someone he'd trained next to for years lying facedown in the dirt in some worthless patch of northern soil –

All of it was for Introvertia, he knew. A quote bubbled to the surface of his mind, something he'd read before: "My death doesn't matter. Introvertia will live, and you will die. Only that matters." Eza's brain fumbled around for several moments trying to place the quote, and at least he had it; the dragon-companion Mazaren had said the phrase to that nameless sorcerer in the book *Heroes of Introvertia*. Eza had been reading that chapter right before he met his first ever Exclaimovian, and his life had never been the same.

But none of that changed the fact that hundreds – thousands? – of Introvertian kids would be waking up the next morning without mothers or fathers. No one who had seen Denavi coming apart in Ezarra's arms could ever rejoice in war, could ever be glad for the violence that came when one nation refused to let another live in peace. Eza knew this wasn't the way he was supposed to be thinking. Introvertia was *winning,* and the kingdom would continue thriving thanks to the noble sacrifices of the men and women Eza hadn't been able to save. The dead had given themselves so others could live, and that counted for something. Didn't it?

Yet the battle wasn't over. The Clairans and Esterians still lurked in the trees, and there was more death to come.

SEVENTEEN

At two in the afternoon, a restlessness came over the Telravian camp, which Eza could detect even from several hundred yards away. He saw Colonel Ennazar rise and begin walking over that direction, so against his better judgment, he made a choice. "Come on," he told Cammie. "I'm going to the Telravian camp."

"Why?" Cammie asked in alarm.

Eza pointed at Colonel Ennazar. "Besides, they're expecting us to be at the battle, he said. We should show them we held up our end of the deal."

"I don't like this," Cammie said. "I don't like this at all."

They caught up with Colonel Ennazar halfway between the Introvertian and Telravian lines. He seemed extremely happy to see them. "Cadets! You've no doubt seen the excitement among the Telravians. I have a suspicion about what may have caused it, and if my guess is correct, then –"

Something like a cold wind blew down from a hill at the rear of the Telravian front line, and a giant stepped to the top. No, not a giant, Eza amended – just a woman, but she was *tall*, nearly six and a half feet. Her face and arms were bare, and a small bit of her legs could be seen between the bottom of her black skirt and the tops of her knee-length boots. Every inch of exposed skin was slashed and scarred, as if she'd dueled a thousand swords at once and lost.

"Arianna," Colonel Ennazar said in awe. "The Queen of the Seven. Not...an actual queen, of course, as Telravia is strictly a meritocracy. But she and her husband are the de facto leaders of the Seven. Whatever they want, they almost always get."

"How do you know so much about the Seven?" Cammie asked.

"They say," continued Colonel Ennazar as if she hadn't spoken, "that Arianna even has power over the dead. For her to be here is really something. It's said that she rarely leaves the Forsaken Citadel."

"Who says it?" Cammie pressed again.

"One has to know these things about one's allies," Colonel Ennazar said dismissively. "Regardless, her presence on the battlefield is very significant. It means Telravia is afraid they might lose. There's no way they would risk having her here otherwise."

"They think we might lose?" Eza repeated in fear.

"We won't. Not with Arianna here."

The Queen of the Seven strode forward, her presence seeming to draw the warmth out of the air around her. Eza got the impression she was surveying everything around her, and then her eyes locked on his. Even from such a distance, Eza could feel her sizing him up, as if she were evaluating the magical power in him. Her eyes lingered on him, then on Cammie for an even longer time, then on Colonel Ennazar before looking back out over the battlefield. Eza didn't know what was about to happen, but he was sure it would be *bad*.

Arianna had arrived just in time. The Clairan army burst out of the far trees again, leading the way with a volley of fireballs that sent Telravian sorcerers hurtling into the afternoon sky. Purple lances answered, blowing craters in the soil and ripping apart the Clairans at the front of the charge. But the Clairan assault kept coming, and in moments the two front lines had met. The force of the Clairan charge seemed unstoppable, and the Telravian lines started to collapse backward. Physical combat was definitely not their strength.

At that moment the Esterians came charging as well, blasting their own primal lances at the Introvertians, who answered with elemental magic. Eza took Cammie by the hand and sprinted back toward the Introvertian lines. If Colonel Ennazar wanted to be so close to Arianna, that was his business, but Eza wanted no part of it.

Only when he and Cammie were safe again did Eza reopen his mind link to Aleiza. The dragon was holding position behind the Introvertian lines, and on the signal from Eza, she swooped down, but alone this time. The other dragon-companions must have been under orders to keep their dragons in reserve. If Aleiza flew in alone, the only target in the sky, she'd be taken down for sure...

Eza tried to force his mind to stay calm. Reaching out through the mind link, he wrapped light around Aleiza and watched as she shimmered into near-invisibility. A faint shining outline was still visible; Eza didn't know whether it was because of the distance or because she was moving quickly, or if he just wasn't good enough at Artomancy yet, but that was the best he could do. Hopefully the Esterians wouldn't know what they were seeing.

"Did you do that?" Cammie asked as she watched Aleiza blink out of sight.

Eza wanted to reply, but the effort of keeping Aleiza invisible through the mind link was almost overwhelming. It was *way* harder than maintaining the spell on himself, and he didn't know why. He hoped he didn't end up exhausted like Cammie did when she overextended herself. He fed Aleiza all the power he could, and watched through her eyes as she hurtled down toward the charging Esterians.

Suddenly there was fire *everywhere*, and for a moment Eza panicked, wondering if the Esterians had hit Aleiza with a fireball – but no, they were primal spellcasters, not elemental – and then Aleiza's outline shimmered up away from the Esterian troops. Eza could feel Aleiza's intense pride; *she* had made that fireball, although she'd drained an awful lot of Eza's energy in the process. He sat down hard, faintly feeling Cammie's hand on his shoulder. "Are you alright?" she asked, the concern in her voice bordering on fear.

"Fine," he croaked, as Aleiza banked in for another attack. Eza groaned from the strain as Aleiza drew even more magical energy through the link and torched the Esterian rear once again. Scorpion shells popped and burst in the heat and Eza could sense Aleiza's nostrils filling with the scent of roasted wolf hair.

But Aleiza had drawn too much. Eza didn't have any more to give. Aleiza's invisibility flickered, and suddenly she was visible, just yards above the Esterians.

Instantly the sky filled with arrows and purple lances. Aleiza's incredible speed carried her back over the Introvertian front line, heading toward Eza, and the Introvertian spellcasters sent spears of electricity arcing toward the distracted Esterians. Aleiza was almost back to Eza when a single purple lance caught her under the ribcage. She tumbled out of the sky and crashed to the ground only a few feet from Eza.

"No!" he shouted, scrambling to his feet and sprinting the few steps to Aleiza. She would live, right? She would be okay. Denavi had taken a primal lance to the stomach and lived; she had healed herself. Eza could heal Aleiza too. He had to.

With fear strangling him, he had a hard time concentrating, especially on a spell he didn't know very well and had never properly trained. He saw Aleiza in front of him, but some part of his mind kept seeing her close her eyes and not open them again, kept seeing himself return home without a dragon, kept feeling emptiness as he looked out the back door and she wasn't in the garden –

She's not dead, but she will be if you don't pull it together, he told himself.

Eza reached out with all the energy he had, searching for the broken places inside Aleiza, the organs that had been pierced by magic. He could see blood and torn flesh, and he pushed in with growth magic, rejoining the ripped pieces. Aleiza whined and struggled, but Eza urged her to stay still, and Aleiza put her head back down. The sounds of battle faded in his ears; nothing existed except for that jagged hole in Aleiza. Slowly, methodically, he knit together layer after layer of her body. At last he reached her scaly skin. Several of the scales had been shattered, but Eza drew her skin together and healed it as best he could. Over and over the spot he went, but an ugly pockmarked scar remained, just like the one Denavi had on her stomach. Maybe that was the best he'd be able to do, Eza thought; perhaps there was just something about this magic that couldn't be healed all the way.

Aleiza's discomfort seemed to be ebbing, and Eza stood up, letting her rest. He was ferociously hungry but nauseous at the same time – which meant he now knew how Cammie felt when she used too much magic. Great. That meant he had overextended himself. If the battle went sour and Introvertia needed to retreat quickly, Eza couldn't be sure he'd have the strength.

"I need food," he told Cammie, his throat feeling like it would rip apart from dryness.

Cammie reappeared a few moments later with some bread and fruit juice, which Eza downed in seconds, praying he didn't throw it all up again. "Thanks," he told Cammie. "You're the best."

"Don't forget it," she teased. "Are you sure you're okay?"

"Fine. I think. I did too much at once."

Cammie opened her mouth to reply but slammed her hands over her ears instead. The Telravians were wailing again; the Clairans had pushed them hard and their front line had retreated almost all the way to Arianna. The Queen of the Seven towered above all the rest of her soldiers, yet no Clairan magic or arrows could seem to touch her. She joined in the wail, harmonizing with the sound made by her soldiers. As she did, a pale gray fog seemed to spring up from the ground, billowing out to envelop the Telravians, then the Clairans. The shrieks of fear and panic that came from the Clairan troops were far more terrifying than anything the Telravians had ever done. Eza didn't know what that fog was doing, but he was about to find out, because it was pouring this way.

In seconds it had wrapped itself around him, ice cold like death itself, churning with a kind of dark energy that Eza had never felt before – like death itself was trying to grab hold of his insides and carry him away. Cammie was screaming in his ear, wrapping her arms tightly around him as if he could protect her from the horror somehow. But maybe he could –

Eza pushed back outward with light magic, building a blanket of bright warmth around him and Cammie and Aleiza. He held Cammie as closely as he could, straining his sight to see outside. It looked to him like the fog was rippling toward the Clairans and Esterians, passing through Esterian troops who screamed uncontrollably, wisping through Clairans who turned in panic and began stabbing their comrades. "Power over the dead," Ennazar had said – was this what death magic looked like? Was Arianna siphoning the life force from her enemy to make herself stronger? Eza didn't even care whether Arianna won the battle for them; if this was what she brought to the field, Eza wanted none of it.

Cammie's screaming had subsided to whimpers, and Eza pulled her head into his neck, trying to hide the horror from her. He could sense the fog rolling over his cocoon, radiating hopelessness and doom. It was tempting to push back with more light, to try and use his magic to cover more people, but he was already over-exhausted and didn't want to risk wearing himself out and having his bubble collapse. He just clung to Cammie, hoping against hope that it would soon be over.

At last the fog dissipated and complete silence descended on the battlefield. The Esterians and Clairans had fled in terror; there was no sign of them in the woods. The Introvertians seemed to have been physically unharmed by the fog, but all of them had blank looks on their faces, as if they'd peered straight into death itself and been overwhelmed by what they saw.

Bodies lay *everywhere,* Clairan and Telravian and Introvertian and Esterian alike, sprawled over the top of each other. That was *a lot* of kids going to sleep tonight without moms and dads, Eza thought. He couldn't look anymore. Turning away, he buried his head on Cammie's shoulder and tried not to cry.

As the afternoon stretched on, it sure seemed like the battle was over. Dragon scouts had seen the Clairans fleeing northeast to their own kingdom and the Esterians were streaming, disorganized, back toward Mistal. The Introvertians could have pursued them, could probably have made the victory even more decisive than it already was, but General Nazoa ordered the troops to stay put. Four thousand Introvertian soldiers had died in a single day of fighting, one out of every ten who'd marched from Tranquility, and thousands more were wounded. Five hundred dragons were dead, too, their companions already grieving. The Telravian forces had been hit even harder; nearly twenty thousand of their soldiers had been killed, almost forty percent of their entire army. The Clairans and Esterians...

It almost wasn't even possible to see the ground between the Telravian lines and the forest because of how many Clairans had died. Early estimates were that forty thousand of them were gone, over a third of their entire army. The Esterian casualties were harder to count, spread as they were across several miles of plains and forest, but they appeared to have lost more than fifteen thousand. The victory had been decisive for Introvertia, and Eza should have been rejoicing. The people who started the battle had lost it, and would probably be in no condition to start another one anytime soon. The Introvertians, who'd been unjustly attacked, had won. But Eza couldn't stop thinking of the Clairans and Esterians – and even Telravians, although he had a much harder time summoning sympathy for those – who would never be getting their friends or their loved ones back.

All because Exclaimovia had stolen Introvertia's dragons and had threatened a war to cover their own disgrace. Eza couldn't help shaking his head at the injustice. All of this over pride. All of this because Exclaimovia was trying to save face.

The Telravians were already gone, following Arianna back toward the Forsaken Citadel. Colonel Ennazar came hustling up to Cammie and Eza. "I've been told to convey Queen Arianna's gratitude to you. She was most satisfied that we brought our magical ambassadors with us, and she looks forward to seeing you at any future battles in which our sides join forces."

"Excuse me?" Cammie asked, repulsion evident on her face. "She expects us to what, now?"

"My conversation with her was extremely brief, but it seems that she is impressed with your magical potential. She believes that if Introvertia is cultivating spellcasters with your level of power – and with mine, of course – then we will remain worthy allies of Telravia."

"Gross," said Cammie. "I don't see what she needs us for anyway, if she can do *that*." Cammie waved her hands in the air, as if gesturing at the dissipated fog.

"Arianna is not invincible. There are limits even to her power, great though it may be." Colonel Ennazar looked at Eza. "She was most intrigued at the way you were able to repel the fog's effects through your own magic."

Eza didn't reply.

"At any rate," Colonel Ennazar said, "we did what we came to do. You survived and you impressed the Telravians. Well done. I'll be sure to commend you to General Leazan upon our return to Carnazon."

He moved away again, and Cammie watched him go. "Is it bad that I really, really don't want to impress the Telravians?" she asked.

"No. Whatever those people like, I want the exact opposite."

"Me too." Cammie took Eza's hand. "Thanks for protecting me from the fog earlier. I was really scared."

"Anything for you."

"Anything?" Cammie asked, tilting her head with a smile.

"I said what I said," Eza told her, unable to help from grinning back.

"Good. Because I'm almost finished writing my next play, so you'll have lines to memorize when we get back to Tranquility."

"I can't wait."

The Wind Before Rain

EIGHTEEN

Eza had insisted that Introvertians didn't *mob,* but there was no other explanation for what happened when Cammie and Eza came through the south gate of Carnazon on Friday morning. If Cammie thought that she and Eza had experienced the most interesting weeks in the history of Carnazon before, things had only gotten crazier now that the two of them had been a part of Introvertia's largest battle in centuries. Of course, Cammie hadn't done very much in the battle, since she hadn't wanted to draw attention to herself and attract attention from enemy archers or sorcerers, but she had been there, and *oh yes,* she had stories to tell.

Some stories, of course. She didn't particularly want to think any further about the Telravian death mist, and she'd had her face planted in Eza's neck so hard that she hadn't seen much of it anyway, but it was kind of impossible to tell the story of the battle without it, so Cammie supposed she would have to.

They were nearly late to Professor Ozara's history class because of how many times Cammie had to stop and tell some version of the story to a student who asked, but that wasn't the last of it. When they finally did take their seats, Professor Ozara looked warmly at

Cammie. "In this class you've learned about many different events from history, but it's not every day that my students help *make* history. All of you have heard about the battle that took place on Tuesday, which we're calling the Battle of Denneval Plain. Most of what you've heard has been secondhand, but Cadet Ravenwood and Cadet Skywing witnessed it in person. I'd like for them to share what they saw."

Cammie followed Eza to the front of the classroom, and Professor Ozara took the seat Eza had just vacated. Cammie nearly giggled; it was funny to be at the front of the class lecturing the professor. Eza motioned to her as if offering her the floor, so Cammie stepped forward and told the story.

She spent the next hour going over every detail: how the Clairans and Esterians had hid in the forests, the Esterian feint at the Introvertian flank, the dragons and scorpions and wolves, and Arianna and the death mist and the frantic retreat of Introvertia's enemies. Cammie noticed with pride that all of the students were listening with rapt attention – all except Razan and Anneka, who were deliberately pretending to be uninterested.

How petty can you be, she thought to herself, not breaking her stride as she concluded the story and bowed to Professor Ozara.

If she'd thought that would be the last she'd have to

talk about it, she was *extremely* mistaken. Since she'd used the entire hour-long class, there hadn't been time for questions, so as soon as Professor Ozara dismissed the class, a large blob formed around Cammie and Eza at the front of the class.

"I thought you said Introvertians didn't mob," she teased Eza.

"Is this really a mob, or is it more of a blob?"

"Maybe later you can explain the difference."

"Well, a mob means you're right, and a blob means I'm right, so..."

Cammie laughed. "So it's like that, then."

Another hour passed by as they answered questions from their excited classmates – even though it meant all of them were skipping Professor Grenalla's Survivalship class. No detail went unexplored; these Introvertians were sponges of knowledge, Cammie thought in amusement. The closest she'd ever come to seeing one Introvertian interrupt another was when they all opened their mouths to ask something at once, and then immediately all began deferring to each other. Cammie would never stop being entertained by their faultless politeness.

Eventually Eza apologized and said that it was lunchtime, which didn't seem to bother the others too much; it appeared most of their questions had been answered. Cammie followed Eza out the classroom door and turned right toward the staircase down to the mess hall. Razan and Anneka were waiting for them. "Ooooh, look," Razan said bitterly. "Everyone loves the Exclaimovian. Maybe we should just throw open the city gates and invite them all in."

"Please tell me you didn't wait there an entire hour just to harass us when we walked by," Cammie said. "That would be sad."

"This isn't about me. This is about all the people at Carnazon who don't think you should be here."

"And yet it's only ever you two giving us a hard time," Cammie snapped. "Are you saying all your friends are too cowardly to say it to our faces?"

"They're too *polite,*" corrected Anneka. "But someone needs to say it. You should leave the school. You don't even have a dragon."

Suddenly Eza was laughing. Cammie didn't understand why, but it seemed to *really* bother Anneka and Razan, so she didn't say anything. "You're so jealous," Eza said at last. "You're like a little kid who's upset that his older brother got a better toy on the Day of Lights. You're sulking and throwing a temper tantrum because people would rather hear Cammie's stories than hang out with you. Here's an idea. Maybe if you went and did interesting things with your lives, instead of trying to make this place miserable for someone who's only ever been nice to you, people might want to hear your stories too."

"I don't think you –" Razan began.

"There's no *thinking* involved," Eza cut him off. Cammie had finally seen it! She'd seen one Introvertian interrupt another – and it had been EZA! She really was rubbing off on him, but she couldn't gloat just now, so she settled for wearing an enormous smirk instead. Eza continued, "Cammie is a student here at the direct order of the king. Are you saying the king made a mistake?"

Razan was silent; he looked to Anneka for guidance, but she said nothing.

"Are you saying the king made a mistake?" Eza repeated.

Cammie loved watching Razan squirm. If he said no, he would have to admit Cammie was at the school legitimately. If he said yes...well, that would be *very* interesting to a number of people in authority at Carnazon, and in the palace. An Academy student second-guessing direct orders from the king was not going to end well.

But the seconds stretched on and Razan stubbornly refused to say anything one way or the other.

"Let's go," Cammie told Eza. "I'm hungry." She locked elbows with him and led him toward the staircase, not looking back.

After a lunch of sausage and salad, Cammie turned to Eza. "If we were going to put on a play here, where would be the best place?"

"Probably the east side function room, where they have the formal dances in the spring."

"Great! Let's go practice there."

"Actually, that room is used for fifth-year Artomancy lessons on Friday afternoons. We'll have to find somewhere else, or wait for them to be finished."

Cammie's one brown and one blue eye lit up with a smile. "I don't want to wait. Let's find an empty room."

"What about the eastern guard tower?"

"Perfect!"

So up they climbed to the tower, and Cammie fished the script out of her backpack. "I only have the one copy," she warned, "so don't let any pages go flying away, okay?"

"Okay." Eza took the script carefully, examining the title page. "*The Ranger's Dilemma,*" he read aloud. "It's about a Ranger. I like it already."

"Read your lines," Cammie encouraged him. She'd already memorized all her own lines – in fact, her mind wouldn't let her forget them – so she could quote them back to Eza while he read from the script.

The play was about a student who was studying to be

a Ranger when he found that he had to make a choice. On one hand was the future he'd always planned for himself, and on the other was his love for a friend who could be more than a friend. Eza shouldn't have been surprised by this, she thought. He was the one who said he'd give up his dreams "to have a love people wrote poems about," the line Cammie had stopped to write down immediately on hearing it, and the line that formed the entire basis of the play. The further they got into their rehearsal, the faster her heart was beating.

He had absolutely no idea what was about to happen to him, Cammie thought...

After an hour of reading, they reached the climax of the play, in which the Ranger named Nezala chose true love over the life he'd planned, and then kissed the woman he loved, Kiranna. Cammie's heart was thundering now as Eza looked up from the pages of the script. "The characters kiss?" he clarified.

"People kiss in theater all the time," Cammie said, sounding more defensive than she'd meant to. "It doesn't have to mean anything. But...it's more convincing if you do mean it."

Eza stared at her for several moments, as if thinking over what she'd said. "Well, if the script says it..."

Cammie couldn't believe it was actually working. He was really going to kiss her! Her knees shook so hard she almost fell over as Eza took the last few steps toward her, put one hand on the side of her face and the other on her back, and...

Their lips met, and Cammie felt herself wrapping her arms around Eza. All the subtle hints he hadn't noticed, all the teasing jokes he hadn't seen through, all the head massages that hadn't turned into anything more, all of them had been worth it for this moment. Introvertians really *didn't* take hints, she thought, but they would apparently take stage direction.

Yet this was no theater kiss; there was passion in it, excitement, and when Eza finally pulled back, the giant smile on his face was unmistakable. "You said it's better if I mean it," he said apologetically. "Well...I meant it."

"I think we should rehearse that part again," Cammie suggested. "Just, you know, to make sure it's perfect."

"Okay," Eza said. "Let me go back to where the script says I should be."

He was really treating it like it was just a play! Cammie was mad for half a second until she looked over at Eza and saw the mischievous grin on his face. He knew exactly what he was doing; he was just teasing her.

"I'd give up all my dreams for love," Eza said, his eyes locked on Cammie's, the script forgotten on the floor by his feet. "But I wouldn't be giving up anything, not really, if it meant I gained a love people write poems about."

And then he crossed the three steps toward Cammie and lifted her off the ground as he kissed her. She put both hands on the sides of his head, never wanting the kiss to end, and when Eza finally set her down, she was so ecstatic she could think of nothing except his lips against hers.

Eza took her by the hands and looked deeply into her eyes. "Will you marry me?" he asked.

"WHAT?!" screeched Cammie.

"It's the next line in the script, you goof," Eza explained. "Nezala asks Kiranna to marry him and she says yes."

"Oh...right. I was...uh, improvising," she said.

They stared at each other for several awkward moments. "I've never kissed anyone before," Cammie blurted.

"Me neither," said Eza. "I'm glad you were my first."

"I'm glad you were mine."

"You know, I'm not sure if you noticed or not, but Nezala's name is almost identical to mine. The N is just at the beginning instead of at the end, and there's an A where there should be an E."

Yes, that's the entire point, Cammie thought to herself. *TAAAAAAKE THE HIIIIIIINT.*

What she said was, "Oh. That's interesting."

Eza smiled at her. "We should take it again from the top."

Eza had lost count of how many times they'd "rehearsed the kissing scene." Every time it was like lightning from his hair down to his toes. And the look in Cammie's eyes, the incredible awe and childlike glee every single time he'd pulled away from her...that was intoxicating.

He knew she *had* to be wondering why he hadn't courted her yet. Something had changed when they'd kissed each other, though. They'd walked home shoulder to shoulder like always, but there was just a little *more* in every brush of his arm against hers. They'd hugged goodnight like always, but the hug had lingered, and Cammie's breath against his neck had been warm and inviting and he hadn't wanted to let go. Cammie had disappeared up the stairs, followed shortly by Denavi, but then Denavi had come back down a few minutes later, lying across one of the sofas with her bare feet propped up on the back.

"I hear you and Cammie had a good afternoon," Denavi teased.

Eza sighed happily. "Today is the best day I can ever remember, Denavi. I kissed Cammie and it was incredible. I mean, we danced together at the Spring

Equinox Festival and that was the best day of my life, but this beat it by a million. The way her..." He trailed off. "I could go into *significant* detail, but I doubt you want to hear it."

"If it's important to you then I want to hear it."

"Hey, that's good. You'll be a true Introvertian in no time."

"That's twice now you've changed the topic on me," Denavi said seriously. "Talk to me about Cammie. Why aren't you courting her yet?"

That drew a very different kind of sigh from Eza. "I want to, Denavi. You have no idea how badly I want to. But I just..."

"You're cautious and scared," she said helpfully.

"Yeah. That exactly." Eza took a deep breath. "I mean, courting isn't like dating. Introvertians don't casually date people and then break up and date someone new. A courting relationship is supposed to end in marriage. It's a promise to court until both people feel ready, and then get married. I'm asking her for a huge commitment."

"Does she know what courting is?"

"Oh, of course. I've told her all about our customs."

"So if you asked her to court, she'd know exactly what she was agreeing to."

"Yes, she would."

"Then don't you owe her the chance to make the

choice herself? To at least ask her and let her decide?"

"But it's not just that." Eza sat back on the sofa, worry written all over his face. "What if Exclaimovia calls a truce tomorrow and she decides to go back home to her family? How could I give my heart away to someone who might be gone the next day?"

"None of us know the future," Denavi told him, gentleness in her voice. "You can't let fear of what-might-be paralyze you. If Ezarra knew your mother was going to die, do you think he still would have married her?"

"Oh, no question. They loved each other madly."

"Do you love Cammie madly?"

Eza stared at her for a second, then nodded. "I love her so much," he said, his voice breaking. "I love every moment we spend together. I love her smile, and her laugh, the way her nose wrinkles when she giggles. I love the way she teases me, the way she gets so excited that she interrupts me. I love every single thing about her, Denavi."

"Then why would you let that slip away from you?" Denavi whispered.

Eza nodded, over and over again, slowly. "Okay," he said. "When we perform the play, I'll ask her. Right at the very end. That's the kind of special moment I think she'd love. Don't tell her, though. I want it to be a surprise."

"I won't tell her," promised Denavi.

The faintest flicker of movement from the bottom of the staircase caught Eza's eye. If he hadn't been a Ranger, if he hadn't spent years training himself to notice the smallest possible details, he would have thought it was just his imagination. But he was sure he'd seen something.

And that made him smile.

NINETEEN

A messenger from the king came the next morning to announce that Denavi's house arrest had been lifted. The tactics she'd provided to the Introvertian army had turned the tide of battle; without Denavi's information, General Nazoa would have shifted the Introvertian lines to meet the Esterian assault on their right flank, and Claira would have charged directly at their weakened left side. Without that movement, Claira had been forced into a costly frontal attack on the Telravians instead.

The messenger had also brought a declaration that Denavi was a guest of the crown, and that she was free to move about the city, to buy or sell goods, and get a job if she pleased. "I guess I'll need to do something eventually," Denavi mused. "I'll be finished reading all your books in a couple of weeks at this rate."

"Bring some with you," Eza encouraged, sitting next to Cammie while the two of them ate breakfast. "Let's go down to the Reading Square."

So Denavi led the way out the front door, and Eza breathed in the cool warmth (an odd phrase, thought Eza, but the air was cool while the sun on his face was warm) of the spring morning. Denavi stopped a few steps into the street, smiling at a man who walked by pushing a cart of freshly baked bread. "You have a really nice smile," she told him.

"Thank you!"

Eza elbowed Cammie. "See? She's getting it."

Cammie pretended to gag. "Accepting compliments from one person is hard enough."

Eza put his hand on the back of her neck, spinning her toward him. Behind her glasses, her split-colored eyes were shining. "You have a really nice smile, too," he told her.

"Stop. You're going to make me blush."

"Then blush. You're beautiful and you should know it."

Eza had been expecting a protest, but something odd seemed to happen inside Cammie, as if she were about to argue with him but then suddenly decided she didn't want to. "Thank you," she said. "I don't know why I told you to stop. I like when you say nice things about me. But...like, one or two at a time. I'm still getting used to it."

"One or two at a time it is."

They continued toward the Reading Square, but when they were almost there, Eza tugged Cammie off to the right. "But the Reading Square is that way," Cammie said, pointing straight ahead.

"I know. We're going to the Music Square."

"You just told Denavi we were going to the Reading Square."

"Did I? I must have misspoken."

Cammie stared at him, her mouth open. "You're planning something."

"Plotting," Eza corrected, unable to hide his grin.

Cammie squealed, drawing a look from a merchant riding a wagon past them. "I! HATE! SUSPENSE!"

"That's why it's so much fun to torture you."

"EEEEEEEEEEEEE."

Eza was sure that Cammie was dying the whole way to the Music Square, but Eza himself was on edge too. From a block away they could hear the sounds of melodies and harmonies from a dozen kinds of instruments plus voices. Eza knew this was Cammie's favorite place in the entire city; the first time she'd seen it, she'd lingered there and he'd practically had to drag her away by the arms. Just the fact that they were going was probably enough to fill her with delight, but when she saw...

Eza led them into the square and then to the right, to a spot where only a few musicians were set up, ballainas in hand. He knew Cammie probably recognized them; there was Inaza Varraen from Sun Company, who was in their Dragon Care class, with a few others. Inaza smiled when he saw them approaching and nudged the others, and they launched into a slow, quiet ballad.

"What's this?" Cammie asked in surprise.

Eza extended his hand. "Would you like to dance with me?"

But Cammie just stood, looking to the musicians and then to Eza. "You did this for me?" she asked quietly.

"Yes," Eza answered, his hand still out. "Now, do you have more questions, or shall we dance?"

"I'm sure I could think of a few more," Cammie smirked as she took Eza's hand and buried her face in his neck.

The two of them swayed back and forth in the cool morning air. The first time they'd danced together, Eza's heart had been thundering from excitement and nervousness. This time, he just felt calm and relaxed. This was *right,* with Cammie in his arms. Eza felt a little embarrassed at how long it had taken him to finally catch on, and he couldn't wait to ask her to court him.

But of course, he *would* wait until the day they performed the play for a real audience.

Before that happened, though...there was one other thing he'd be taking care of later that day.

He and Cammie danced for the entire morning, slow songs and waltzes and trot-steps and whatever else Inaza and his band felt like playing. By lunchtime, Eza was starving, and he knew Cammie probably was, too. "I'll tell you what," he said to Cammie. "Why don't you take Denavi to the Windwhisper restaurant, and then go clothes shopping with her. Shanna never had the chance, so Denavi is still wearing my shirt."

Cammie looked over at Denavi, who had spent the entire morning listening to music and examining the gray stone buildings that bordered the square and smiling at strangers. "She likes Introvertian clothes. Maybe you should be the one to take her."

"I don't want to go clothes shopping. You take her."

With a raised eyebrow, Cammie leaned in. "You're trying very hard to get rid of me. Are you plotting something else?"

"Yes!" Eza exclaimed. "Just take her shopping already and let me go plot!"

Cammie grabbed Eza to keep from falling over in hysterical laughter. "You're blurting whatever is on your mind just like an Exclaimovian would."

Something had clicked in Eza's head when Cammie leaned close to him like that. When she lifted her head, her face was right there, and...

With a hand on the back of her neck, Eza pulled her toward himself, and their lips met again. A look of wonder was in Cammie's eyes when they finally separated. "Wow," she said. "Right here in front of everybody like that."

"They're going to see us kiss in the play soon enough."

"Mmmmm. Good point."

"Now take Denavi shopping and let me plot." Eza held up his hands and drummed his fingers together.

"I have ways of extracting information from you," Cammie threatened.

"You won't have to extract it. You'll find out soon enough."

Cammie gave him what was probably supposed to be a threatening glare, but it only made Eza laugh. "I'll see you back at the house, Cammie."

She led Denavi across the far side of the square, talking loudly about something as she walked. Eza waited until they'd turned a corner and couldn't see where he was going, and then took off toward the Reading Square. His biggest surprise was yet to come.

"Thank you all for coming," King Jazan said to the assembled generals. Cammie and Eza, in their black Academy dress uniforms, were seated in the back of the room; Cammie didn't know exactly why they'd been summoned, but assumed it had something to do with the fact that Telravia considered them to be Introvertia's magical ambassadors. It was Sunday night, and the next morning was the first day of the final week of the term.

Classes at the Academy went for six weeks on followed by two weeks off, and Cammie was excited for a normal week of classes and then for a little vacation.

She was also excited to perform the play. After Eza had returned from his mystery errand, he'd spent the entire rest of the day, and all day Sunday, memorizing his lines, and Cammie was confident that he'd gotten them all down. She'd almost never seen someone commit an entire play to memory so quickly – but then, the whole play was *about him,* after all. All he really had to do was act like himself.

Eza had booked the east side function room for after dinner on Wednesday, and had made it his mission to invite as many people as he could. There was no way to know until that day just how many people would show up for a play written by an Exclaimovian, but Eza seemed optimistic – of course, he always did – so Cammie was hopeful too.

But "hopeful" didn't seem the right word to describe the mood back in the palace's throne room as King Jazan stood next to Queen Annaya. "Anxious" was more like it, or perhaps "tense." The king held out his hand to speak and all the other chatter in the room immediately ceased.

"The war council is now in session," said the king. "We have several significant items on the agenda for tonight. The first is a full after-action report on the battle of the Battle of Denneval Plain. The second is to discuss our long-term strategy for magical training. For the first, I will cede the floor to General Nazoa, who held command for the battle."

General Nazoa stood and gave an extremely detailed account of the battle, which matched up in every way with Cammie's own recollections. She leaned forward in her seat when the general reached the part about Arianna, Queen of the Seven, appearing on the battlefield. Cammie's memories of that part of the battle were hazy; she recalled a fog and then Eza wrapping her in a bubble of light and warmth, but that was it.

"The mist," General Nazoa said, choosing his words carefully, "appeared to be some kind of very powerful death-magic." Audible disgust rippled across the room, and the general held his hand up. "We were no doubt spared the worst of it, so we do not know whether the spell itself affected our enemies or whether the fear of the thing was sufficient to induce panic –"

"The fear of the thing!" repeated Colonel Ennazar in an offended tone, leaping to his feet. "Do you doubt Arianna's power, General? Were you ignorant of what happened to the battle-hardened Clairan troops the moment her death mist touched them?"

All sound in the room ceased. King Jazan stared at Colonel Ennazar in shock. "Colonel, did you just interrupt your superior officer?"

"I will not stand here and let Arianna's name be slandered," Colonel Ennazar said vigorously.

"She used necromancy to win a battle," General Nazoa argued. "That kind of dark magic –"

"She won the battle in a single hour without losing a single life!" snapped Colonel Ennazar. "My king, if we had that same power at our disposal, just *think* of how many Introvertian lives could be saved the next time we found ourselves attacked!"

"We will not launch ourselves down a path of studying dark magic just because we think it may benefit us at some later point," King Jazan insisted. "That kind of thinking is precisely the reason Introvertia was forced to give up magic in the first place. Dark magic presents itself as being purely useful, perfectly innocent, and only reveals its true nature once things are too far gone to reverse course. Surely, Colonel Ennazar, you do not –"

"We would not even have to *use* the magic!" Colonel Ennazar said forcefully. Even Cammie, who was no stranger to interrupting people, felt her jaw drop in astonishment that Ennazar had just interrupted not just General Nazoa, but the *king himself*. "Its mere presence would be a deterrent. Do you truly think Exclaimovia, or Claira, or Esteria, or even Telravia itself would ever *dream* of attacking us if they knew we could unleash that kind of power on them?"

"Preventing that kind of war would save our society from great damage," conceded the king, "but only at the cost of the damage it would cost us if our best and brightest minds spent their time studying how to blur the lines between life and death. Are you honestly suggesting, Colonel, that Introvertia would be a better place, a place more worth saving, if the fifteen hundred students in the Dragon Academy were studying Telravian vampirism rituals instead?" He stared down Ennazar, who for once seemed unwilling to butt in. "Look around you, Colonel, as you walk down the street. The Kingdom of Introvertia is a place where people are honest and kind, where we celebrate life and beauty. That is who we are and that is who we want to be. We could not do what you are suggesting, could not worship death and violence, and remain Introvertia."

"Yet you're content to go running to Telravia for help whenever your pacifism puts your kingdom at risk of destruction," Ennazar said heatedly, and several of the other generals took sharp breaths, as if still in disbelief that a colonel was openly arguing with the king.

"Who is Telravia's greatest poet?" Queen Annaya asked.

Ennazar said nothing.

"Who is their greatest novelist? Their greatest

playwright?" pressed Queen Annaya. "Who are their painters, their sculptors? They don't produce beauty, Colonel. Their society revolves around nothing except the pursuit of magical power. Is that what you want Introvertia to become?"

"Art means nothing if your kingdom is destroyed in battle," Ennazar said, but it seemed to Cammie that his protest was halfhearted, as if he knew he wasn't going to win.

"Winning in battle means nothing if your kingdom isn't worth fighting for," Queen Annaya told him.

Colonel Ennazar sat back down, looking around the throne room as if trying to see whether he'd changed any minds.

"That provides a nice transition into our second agenda item," King Jazan said smoothly, "that of our preparation for the next phase of the war, whatever it may hold for us. I was going to announce the promotion of Colonel Aric Ennazar to general, and assign him to his new post as the director of military magic, but in light of the colonel's recent outburst, I will be reconsidering that decision. Generals, please submit to me your recommendations for that position as soon as possible. It is no small task to train forty thousand soldiers in battlefield magic and to ensure that we adapt our tactics to make use of those abilities. However, if our dragon-companions in particular can train their magic, and the dragons can become larger and stronger as a result, then our aerial strength alone may win a number of fights for us." The king stared pointedly at Ennazar. "That is how we will win. We will rely on each other and on our friendship with our dragons. It is trust and hard work that will see us through, not turning ourselves into a copy of Telravia. You say we need to win in order to protect the kingdom, but if the only way to win is to compromise our values, then we will not be protecting Introvertia at all. We would lose everything that our ancestors worked and fought and died to preserve. We will win as Introvertia, and our way of life will carry on."

Cammie fought the urge to applaud, and if even one of the generals had started, she would absolutely have joined in. As it was, King Jazan dismissed the war council, and the generals filed out of the room. Eza stayed put, waiting for the room to empty, and then the king motioned him and Cammie up to the throne. "I have to apologize to you, Ezalen," the king said. "When you first warned me about Colonel Ennazar and his reaction to Arianna, I didn't believe you. Please understand that I wasn't questioning your integrity. I thought perhaps you were confused or had misunderstood the colonel's disposition. Now, of course, none of the generals have any doubt about how much he idolizes Telravia."

Cammie was staring at Eza in surprise. "You told the king?" she asked.

Eza nodded. "I wrote everything down before we'd left the battlefield and sent it as soon as we arrived back in town."

"And it took a lot of courage to do so," the king told Eza. "Under normal circumstances, questioning your superior officer is an extremely serious offense, especially if it's done by going straight to the king. But there are certain times when keeping one's mouth closed is the greater wrong."

"'If you know the right thing and don't do it, you've done evil,'" Cammie quoted. "It's an Exclaimovian proverb. I told myself that in my bedroom the night before I left for Introvertia."

"Your people have many good qualities and many wise sayings," King Jazan said with a smile.

That perplexed Cammie, and she stared at him for several moments. "I thought Introvertians hated Exclaimovia."

"Doubtless some do. There is a long and difficult history between our kingdoms, and there is much between us that would have to be resolved before there can be any hope of a permanent peace." He looked back at Queen Annaya, who smiled gently. "I spoke to

Colonel Ennazar about values, the things that make Introvertia unique. When I think of who I want my people to be...I do not want us to be people who hold grudges and cultivate bitterness in our hearts. I want us to be people who long for peace and reconciliation, even with our oldest enemies. I do not know if I have any ability to bring that peace into reality; the choice belongs to Exclaimovia and whether they continue to threaten us with war. But I promise you, Cammaina, I will do what I can for your people."

"My people are here," she told him. "This is home. There are people I love in Exclaimovia, but Introvertia is where I feel welcomed and accepted. You took me in when Exclaimovia kicked me out – for following the words of their own proverb." Cammie looked sideways at Eza. "Besides, there are people I love here, too."

Delight sprang up in her as Eza turned red and looked at the ground to try and hide it. He had no idea, she thought, that she'd been eavesdropping on his conversation with Denavi. Making him blush in front of the king was her revenge on him for taking so long to ask her out.

"I truly hope there will be peace in our days," King Jazan said. "Farewell, Cadets."

TWENTY

Wednesday night arrived at last, and Cammie was nearly beside herself with excitement. There was already a stage at one end of the east side function room, which was normally the bandstand when the room hosted formal dances. Eza, since he was playing a Ranger, had simply dressed in his normal clothes and his Academy cloak. Cammie, in a fit of incredible irony, had needed to borrow some of Denavi's new Introvertian clothes. Eza didn't seem nervous at all, which Cammie didn't think was fair. It made sense, in a way; he'd never performed in front of an audience like this before, except for the soldiers on their march to Telravia, so perhaps he didn't know he was *supposed* to be nervous.

Cammie's eyes were drawn to the door as two uniformed guards came in, then two more, then two more behind them. This was officially strange, she thought. Her eyes almost popped out when she saw the next pair to enter the room: it was King Jazan and Queen Annaya. The queen glanced toward the stage and waved at Cammie, who weakly waved back.

Then Cammie ran to Eza and grabbed him by the shoulders. "DID YOU DO THIS?" she shrieked.

"Do..."

"THE KING AND QUEEN ARE HERE!"

"Ah, yes. Do you remember when I made you take Denavi clothes shopping so I could plot?"

"THIS IS NOT A PLOT, EZA. THIS IS TORTURE. YOU CAN'T JUST DO SOMETHING LIKE THAT ON OPENING NIGHT." Cammie took a deep breath, but it didn't help. "I hate you SO MUCH RIGHT NOW."

"You do not either."

"No," she admitted, "I don't. I shouldn't have said that. It was very kind and thoughtful of you to ask them here. But...EEEEEEEEEEEEEEE."

Eza moved in to hug Cammie, and she let herself be drawn into his arms. "You'll be fine," he assured her.

"Eeeeeee...."

But six o'clock was upon them, and there was no more time to shriek. The show had to go on. Eza had gotten Shanna to give a brief introduction to the play, and then the lights were coming up – some of Eza's Artomancy classmates had agreed to take turns using their light magic on the stage so it would be brighter – and the curtain was pulled to the side. Instantly Cammie transformed. No longer was she Cammaina Ravenwood. For the next forty-five minutes, she was Kiranna Azalan.

The plot was tightly constructed, Cammie knew. Act one established Nezala as a well respected student with dreams of becoming a Ranger, to follow in his father's and grandfather's footsteps. Near the end of act one, he met Kiranna, and his world turned upside down. He spent the entirety of act two being torn between his feelings for Kiranna and his devotion to duty, while Kiranna tried to balance her feelings for him and her family's desire for her to marry another man. Act three was where Kiranna finally made up her mind to tell Nezala that she wanted to marry him, only to be met on the way by Nezala himself making the same declaration to her.

The climax of the play was on top of them, the part she and Eza had practiced the most. He had done a very convincing job so far, had been loud at all the right times and quiet and brooding at all the right times. The stone walls and ceiling had carried his voice all the way to the rear of the room, Cammie knew, and the two of them had the crowd leaning in expectantly.

"I'd give up all my dreams for you...for love," Eza declared urgently. He'd goofed up the line, Cammie noticed, but he kept right on going, just as she'd told him. "But I wouldn't be giving up anything at all, not really." His voice caught in his throat, and tears came to the corners of his eyes as he hoarsely croaked the end of the line: "If I gained a love that people wrote poems about."

THAT was unexpected, but the crowd *loved* it. The script called for Eza to come and kiss her, but Cammie couldn't wait for him to arrive. She leaped the three steps to Eza and threw herself into his arms. He caught her effortlessly and they kissed, and it was the single most perfect moment Cammie could ever remember. She was dimly aware of thunderous applause from the crowd, but her eyes were closed and all that existed was Eza and her. At last he began to pull away, and Cammie opened her eyes to see Eza's face just inches from hers. "I love you," he said.

The squeal that erupted from Cammie's mouth was drowned out by the crowd, and she buried her face in Eza's shoulder, unable to let go of him. The applause kept going, with Eza waiting patiently for the chance to deliver his next line. Once the crowd saw the two of them looking at each other, the clapping subsided just in time for Eza to take her hands, smile at her, and ask, "Will you marry me, Kiranna?"

The crowd's deafening cheer seemed like it was going to shake the entire Academy apart. Cammie shouted "YES!" knowing the crowd couldn't hear her, but the way she hurled herself at Eza left the crowd no doubt what her character's answer had been.

At the end of that climactic scene, she and Eza clasped hands and faced the crowd for their bow. Cammie's mouth hurt from smiling. As excited as she was to talk to the audience, especially to see if Queen Annaya had liked her play, part of Cammie just wanted to be out of there so she could get alone with Eza. This next part made her more nervous than performing the play had; she'd been eavesdropping that night he'd talked to Denavi, and she knew he was going to ask her to court him...

If she didn't die from excitement and anticipation first.

Several dozen people stuck around to give personal congratulations to her and Eza, and she was surprised to see the king and queen among them, patiently waiting at the back of the line like normal people. At last Cammie was standing face to face with Queen Annaya, who looked almost as proud as Cammie felt. "Ezalen tells me you wrote that play yourself," the queen said approvingly.

"He gave me the idea, and the line about a love people write poems about."

"Cammie did everything else, though," Eza chimed in.

Queen Annaya smiled. "He also tells me you want to start a theater company here at the Academy. I want you to know you have my full blessing. I'll support you however I can."

"REALLY?" Cammie shouted, and without thinking, she wrapped her arms around the queen.

But Queen Annaya was used to the stage herself, and if she had been surprised, she'd simply improvised the way any good actress would, returning Cammie's hug with a bright smile. "Of course. Ezalen here did a very brave thing by asking us to attend tonight. You should cherish him."

"Oh, I plan to."

King Jazan offered Cammie a hug as well, which she took gratefully. For an Introvertian – and the king of all Introvertians, at that – to initiate physical contact was really meaningful, and Cammie appreciated the gesture. "Your talent is impressive," the king told Cammie. "I believe you will be a truly great playwright one day. Perhaps your art will even be the bridge that brings peace back to our two nations."

"I would love nothing more," Cammie said.

At last the final spectator had left the function room, which by now was nearly dark except for a few torches burning on the side walls. The silence, punctuated only by crackling of fire, felt unusual after hours of acting and applause and chatter afterward. Eza was looking out one of the east-facing windows, lost in thought. Everything inside Cammie was screaming at her to say something to him, to get him talking so he could ask her out, but she held her tongue.

Moments later Eza turned around and came to stand

next to Cammie, taking her hands in his own. "I don't know when I fell in love with you, Cammie. There wasn't one moment where I suddenly realized I was in love. I just...slowly started to notice how good I felt when I was with you, and how when you were gone, I felt like something inside me was missing. That was what finally made me stop and admit it to myself, I think. It was that night I woke up around four in the morning from Razan sneezing and spent the next two hours in the lounge, my head snapping up in excitement every time the door to the girls' barracks opened and someone came out, my heart sinking a little bit every time it wasn't you."

Eza took a big breath, looking into Cammie's eyes. "Cammie Ravenwood, I love everything about you. I love your laugh and the way your nose wrinkles when you smile. I love the way you blurt things when you get excited. I love your creative mind. And I'm scared to death right now because I don't know what the future holds. I'm so afraid that our kingdoms will make peace and you'll decide to go back to your family, and I'll be happy for you but it'll leave this giant hole in me. I want you with me forever, Cammie. I don't want to spend a single day apart from you. I never knew I was incomplete until I saw the way you complete me."

"Whatever you're about to say, the answer is yes," she murmured.

"Cammie, will you enter a courtship with me?"

"YEEEEESSSSSSSS," Cammie shouted as loudly as she could, which was very loud indeed. Eza wrapped her up in a hug, and Cammie couldn't resist adding, "IT'S ABOOOOOOUT TIIIIIIIIIME!"

"I was worth the wait," Eza joked.

"Yes," Cammie said seriously. "You were. And are. I don't know what the future holds either, but I want you in it."

They kissed again in the near-darkness of the function room, a long and slow kiss that Cammie never wanted to end. At last she rested her head against Eza's shoulder. "My dad's going to scream when he finds out I'm engaged to an Introvertian."

"He screams all the time anyway."

"Well, that's...true. But you know what I mean."

"We're not exactly engaged, though. The marriage proposal comes later."

"You mean you get to do something like this again?" Cammie asked gleefully.

"Oh, yeah. Not right away. For now we just get to enjoy this."

"Mmmm," Cammie said, snuggling against him again. "I can do that."

Denavi had forced herself to stay at the Skywing

house all day long. She had been roaming the entire city every waking moment now that her house arrest had been lifted, and had wanted very badly to attend the play, but she also didn't want her presence to distract from what Eza was planning to do. Instead, Denavi had spent a quiet evening at home, reading in the back garden with her feet propped up on Aleiza like the dragon was a footstool. Aleiza really seemed to enjoy spending time with Denavi; Eza had said dragons fed off magical energy, so maybe Aleiza was absorbing something from her.

Denavi heard laughter from halfway down the block; it had to be Cammie. She leaped up, trying not to disturb Aleiza, but the dragon had heard her companion coming and went winging up over the house to spring on Eza from above. When Denavi rounded the corner, she saw Aleiza perched atop Eza's shoulders – a sight which would have been hilarious if Denavi hadn't been so excited for the news she hoped Eza was about to share.

She didn't have to wait long. "EZA ASKED ME TO COURT HIM!" exclaimed Cammie, springing forward and wrapping Denavi in a surprisingly strong hug.

"I'm so happy for you," Denavi told her. "Congratulations. May all your dreams come true, except for one."

Cammie tilted her head, perplexed. "What does that

mean?"

"A great philosopher from my nation, a man named Gemmell, said that. If all your dreams came true, you would have nothing left to live for, nothing to work toward. My hope for both of you is that you have success in everything, except for one thing, so you always have a reason to wake up in the morning."

Eza nodded thoughtfully. "I like that."

Then the front door was opening and Ezarra was peeking his head out. "I thought I heard my favorite Exclaimovian," he said, and Cammie ran toward him with a delighted squeal, her arms out for a hug. "Whoa," Ezarra said, laughing. "That's the first time you've ever given me a hug rather than grudgingly accepting one."

"EZA ASKED ME TO COURT HIM!" she shouted again.

Ezarra pulled away from Cammie and looked at his son. "Good job," Ezarra said quietly. "I'm proud of you."

Eza went toward him for another of those hugs that made Denavi jealous, but she also knew it had been a long time in the making. "Come on," Ezarra said, "this deserves a celebration, and I know just the place."

After a ten-minute walk they were all seated together at the Juniper Glade restaurant, stars beginning to peek out in the sky as the last of the sunlight fled westward. The restaurant itself was a small kitchen building with tables and chairs arranged outside, on the corner of Mazaren Avenue (which ran from the Music Square to the fortress by the same name) and Ajrera Boulevard. Even at this late hour the tables were mostly full, and the murmur of earnest conversations made for soothing background noise. Denavi smiled as Cammie scooted her chair next to Eza and leaned her head on his shoulder. He protectively put his arm around her side and let his head rest against hers. They really were perfect for each other, Denavi thought.

Ezarra had ordered them a family-style meal of light and fluffy bread rolls followed by skewers of kenava meat and grilled vegetables. Every flavor was a surprise and a wonder to Denavi; her taste buds had gotten used to Ezarra's cooking, but these spices were new and unexpected, and Denavi couldn't get enough of them. The days were getting warmer now that the spring equinox had passed, although the nights still had a chill to them. The food on the table was almost gone when a cool wind from the east caught the back of Denavi's neck just right and sent shivers up her whole body. Ezarra put his arm on her shoulder, rubbing gently to warm her up, and Denavi moved closer to make it easier for him.

Family-style meal, Denavi thought. This was the strangest family she could ever have imagined: an Introvertian boy and an Exclaimovian girl madly in love with each other, and an Introvertian dad who treated a Clairan girl like his own daughter. But it *worked*. It was everything Denavi had never known she needed: a father, and siblings, and a house where she belonged. She didn't know exactly *how* she belonged yet, how exactly she was supposed to make a contribution to Introvertian society. That was the Clairan side of her talking, she knew. Clairans were supposed to *earn* their value, to make themselves useful. Here she was surrounded by people who simply enjoyed having her around, who liked her for who she was rather than for anything she'd done. She didn't have to earn their approval; they gave it freely. That was going to take some getting used to, but Denavi was sure she could manage.

Dragon Academy Magic School Selection

Greetings Cadet,

Today is a historic occasion! Magic has not been taught at the Dragon Academy for almost five hundred years, and it has not been welcome in Introvertian society at large for more than eight hundred. You, Cadet, are about to choose which school of magic you're going to learn, and how you're going to contribute to the might of the Introvertian army. As you know, we are currently at war with Exclaimovia, Claira, and Esteria. Your dragon, and your magic, are absolutely vital to helping us secure victory.

Please be aware that a student's choice of magic school is *permanent* and cannot be changed or revoked; the magic itself will not permit this to happen. Think carefully before you make your selection.

We'll see you in class, Cadet!

ELEMENTAL MAGIC
Professor: Aric Ennazar
Meeting Place: Central courtyard

Elemental mages have access to five main abilities: fire,

water, lightning, ice, and earth. Elemental magic is primarily attack-oriented combat magic, as shown by its best-known spells: the fireball, the lightning arc, and the ice beam. Only strong elemental mages can master the more defensive applications. Elemental mages will primarily be front-line combat soldiers. Elemental magic is the most popular choice at the Academy; approximately 50% of students have declared for elemental so far.

ARTOMANCY MAGIC
Professor: Ranan Norraza
Meeting Place: East side function room

Artomancy is an ancient magic that involves manipulating light to create illusions, change the appearance of objects, and camouflage the spellcaster. It is absolutely not a combat-oriented magic and contains few if any attack spells. Artomancers would be ideally equipped to serve as Rangers or scouts, where their camouflage abilities will be most useful. Artomancy is the second most popular choice at the Academy; approximately 20% of students have declared for Artomancy, almost all of whom are on the Ranger track.

PHYSICAL MAGIC
Professor: Enian Kenzana
Meeting Place: Outside the Tranquility city gates

Physical magic involves moving objects: lifting and moving heavy boulders, clearing debris from disaster sites, and so on. The primary battlefield application of this magic is creating battlefield barricades out of nearby objects, although it can also be used to drag enemy battle-falcons out of the air, to hurl rocks at soldiers – or to hurl the soldiers themselves. Most physical mages will be combat engineers or non-combat personnel, such as diplomats or dragon program office staff. Physical magic is tied with defensive magic as the third most popular choice at the Academy; approximately 15% of students have declared for physical magic.

DEFENSIVE MAGIC
Professor: Gracian Ayzar
Meeting Place: On top of the eastern ramparts of Carnazon

Defensive magic includes spells that provide protection or deflection during combat. Primarily this involves using the spellcaster's power to push back against incoming fireballs or primal lances, redirecting them back at the enemy or harmlessly into the air. Defensive magic is also frequently cast on the walls, doors, and windows of buildings such as Carnazon Fortress, King Jazan and Queen Annaya's palace, and even the city walls and city gates. This is because defensive magic – alone among all the different schools – persists after it is cast, meaning the magical barrier it creates can last for days, weeks, or possibly even years for the strongest defensive mages. Defensive mages are split between battlefield duty and work in the dragon program, and it is tied for the third most popular choice at the Academy; approximately 15% of students have declared for physical magic.

(INFORMATION PURPOSES ONLY)
HEALING MAGIC
Professor: none
Meeting Place: none

It has just recently come to our attention that Claira has trained some of their soldiers in healing magic. Presently there is no one in Introvertia who could serve as a healing magic instructor, but when this situation changes, we will make this school available to students.

Please note that primal magic is not offered as a class at Carnazon.

Remember also, Cadet, that your dragon will become stronger and larger as your own magical power becomes greater. Dedicate yourself to your studies so that you can be the best companion possible!

We are honored to have you and your fellow students here at the Academy. With your hard work and dedication to the kingdom, we will become stronger each day. I have no doubt that in the end, Introvertia will prevail – and you will hold your head high knowing you were among the first great spellcasters.

General Anra Leazan
Director, Dragon Academy
Carnazon Fortress
Tranquility, Introvertia

The Adventure Continues!

Dragons of Introvertia Book Three

A Fury Like Thunder

Introvertia has been victorious at the Battle of Denneval Plain – but that was only one battle, and the shadow of war still hangs over the kingdom...

Magical training continues, and Eza and Cammie's classmates push themselves to master their magical abilities. Eza finds himself fighting against an enemy he can't attack with magic or swords – a mental illness called anxiety.

As the threat of violence lingers, a captured map points the way to an ancient Introvertian fortress in the Impassable Mountains that might contain ancient magical secrets which would turn the tide of the whole war. Cammie and Eza lead a squad to investigate – but one of the squad will not make it back alive...

For updates visit:
DragonsOfIntrovertia.com
Facebook.com/DragonsOfIntrovertia